DANNY ORLIS
AND THE
MYSTERIOUS VISITORS

DANNY ORLIS
AND THE
MYSTERIOUS VISITORS

BERNARD PALMER

Danny Orlis and the Mysterious Visitors
© 2024 by Bernard Palmer
All rights reserved. First edition 1970.
Second edition 2024.

Cover image: Adobe Firefly
Character illustrations: John Ball
Editor: Charlene Miskimen

Aneko Press Youth

www.anekopress.com

Aneko Press, Life Sentence Publishing, and our logos are trademarks of Life Sentence Publishing, Inc.
203 E. Birch Street
P.O. Box 652
Abbotsford, WI 54405

JUVENILE FICTION / Religious / Christian / Action & Adventure
Paperback ISBN: 979-8-88936-060-5
eBook ISBN: 979-8-88936-061-2
10 9 8 7 6 5 4 3 2 1
Available where books are sold

CONTENTS

CHAPTER 1

HEADING FOR MINNESOTA

Spring came early to southern Texas – a soft breeze warmed by a gentle sun, flowers poking up from carefully cultivated beds around the Roper ranch house, and newborn calves wobbling on their uncertain, spindly legs. There was always extra work to do on the Circle-R ranch, plus the routine work of fences to mend and cattle to be moved to new pastures. But, for the first time in many years, Clarence Roper was thinking of other things than the ranch and the work to do. At the first opportunity he went to town and came back to the ranch with a handful of airline schedules and travel brochures. He threw them on the kitchen counter in front of Carmen.

"Here's a little reading material for you in your spare time."

Her eyes gleamed when she saw what he had brought home.

"Clarence! You were serious about going to Guatemala!"

He pulled out a chair and sat down.

"And what makes you think I wouldn't be serious?" he asked.

"There's the work on the ranch, for one thing, and the way you used to talk about what a horrible place it was when Jerry and Rosalita were living there. I didn't think you'd *ever* want to go there."

"I want to go down and see if I was right or wrong." Then the smile left his face. "Seriously, I've had a real yearning to see that place ever since we got squared away with God."

Carmen picked up the brochures as though they were something precious.

"I wish Rosalita and Jerry could know how things are with us now and how happy we've been since we became Christians."

Clarence reached out and picked up one of the brochures.

"I was thinking about that the other day. You know, I don't believe they ever did give up on us, in spite of the fact that we must have looked like lost causes. I'm sure they kept praying for us right to the end."

"I'm sure of it." She opened one of the brochures and began to read. "Have you thought about when we would go?"

"Some time after calving would work out best as far as the ranch is concerned."

She had another question that was even more serious.

"What about Philip and Marie? Will we take them along?"

Clarence's eyes narrowed thoughtfully.

"I'd sure like to, but I wonder if it would be wise. We'll have to stay with missionaries in some of the places we'll be visiting. It might be a burden for four of us to come in on people who might scarcely have room for two."

He was the one who suggested Mrs. Flores.

"You ought to ask her about it, Carmen. She's reliable, and she's here on the ranch. It wouldn't create any problems for either her or us."

The following day Carmen talked with Mack's mother and learned that she was willing to take over the responsibility of the Roper children for a few weeks.

"I am glad to," she said. "It will give me a chance to repay you a little for the nice things you have done for me and my family."

Once the matter of caring for Philip and Marie was settled, Carmen began to plan with growing excitement for the trip to the mission field that had claimed her sister and brother-in-law's lives. She and Clarence sent for their passports and went to town to get the immunization shots that were necessary for them to return to the United States. Finally, everything was in order.

"Well, Carmen," Clarence said, "I guess everything's done that has to be done before we leave. Now all we've got to do is to go to San Antonio and catch the plane."

Carmen would have been as excited as he was except for the fact that she had had a visitor that afternoon. She could not hide her concern.

"I'm afraid it's not going to be quite as easy as that. I was just talking with Mack's mother a little while ago. She got a letter from a relative back home in Mexico this morning. She isn't sure that she's going to be able to stay with us all summer. She may have to go home for a while."

The lanky rancher got to his feet, his eyes reflecting his dismay.

"I'll go out and talk to her," he said. "There's no reason for her to go back to Mexico. She's got a good job and a nice home right here. There's no need for her to leave."

"She said she isn't planning on going unless she has to, and she says that she won't stay any longer than is absolutely necessary, but something has come up in her family back home – some sort of an emergency. They may have to have her come down for a few weeks."

Clarence frowned. "That can't be. She's got a responsibility to us. She can't leave until we get back."

"Now, Clarence." Carmen laid a hand on his arm. "You know how much one's family means to a woman like Mrs. Flores. We can't ask her to stay if she feels that she ought to go back to Mexico for a time."

The lines about his mouth softened.

"I guess you're right, but it might mean that we will have to cancel the trip. We might have trouble getting all of the arrangements rescheduled for the same time."

"I've been afraid of that."

Clarence was silent momentarily.

"Do you suppose they could stay with Danny and Kay Orlis?" he asked.

"I don't know." A frown jerked across her face. "What made you think of them?"

"I just happened to remember that Phil and Marie have been begging us to have the triplets come out and spend at least part of the summer with them. How would it work if we let them go up to Minnesota to see DeeDee and Del and Doug?"

Carmen wasn't so sure she approved.

"It might not be convenient for Danny and Kay to have them at the time we want to go. You know they are awfully busy."

"It wouldn't hurt to write and ask them."

Carmen still hesitated.

"Do you think we know them well enough?"

"Sure we do. I'll get a message off to them tonight."

Danny and Kay got Clarence's message asking if Phil and Marie could come and spend some time with them.

"What do you think, Kay?" Danny was reading the note carefully. "Do you suppose we could take Phil and Marie for three or four weeks this summer?"

She looked up. "I always enjoy having them around, Danny. I think it would be nice to have them come."

"Then I guess it's all settled. You know, I'm real happy to think that Clarence and Carmen feel close enough to us that they feel free to write and ask such a favor of us, don't you?"

It wasn't long after Danny and Kay wrote to the Ropers inviting Phil and Marie to spend the month with them that they flew to Minneapolis. Danny arranged his work so he could have the day off, and they all drove to Minneapolis to meet the plane.

"I can hardly wait!" Doug Davis exclaimed. "It's going to be great to have Phil with us this summer."

"I wish I could have brought Blackie along," Del said. "Nearly every time they write they ask about him."

Kay glanced at Doug and DeeDee and winked. "It seems like a waste of time to show a crow to anybody," she said.

Del bristled. "It may seem that way to you, but I've got another idea. Did you ever hear of another talking crow in this part of Minnesota?" He repeated the question. "Did you?"

"You say he can talk," Kay continued, "but none of us has ever heard him. For all we know, you could be giving us a line."

"He can talk, all right. I've got Barney's word for that. He'll tell you if you don't believe me."

"If he can talk so well," Danny put in, "why don't you show us what he can do? Why don't you bring him in the house for a little demonstration?"

"I will," Del retorted defensively. "I'll give you all a real demonstration when I'm sure that he's ready to do it."

Kay laughed pleasantly.

"Seeing's believing," she reminded him. "When you bring him in and let him talk for me, I'll believe he can do it, Del. Until then, all I can say is that I don't know for sure whether he can say a single word."

"Sure you do. I've told you all the words he can say. Can I help it if he's shy?"

"Shy?" Kay's laughter rang. "Whoever heard of a shy crow?"

"You did. I just told you about one."

"You'll have to give me a demonstration."

Del was exasperated. "All right," he exploded. "If you want a demonstration, I'll give you one. One of these days I'll take you out in the shed with me and give you a demonstration. Then you'll have to believe that Blackie can talk."

Danny was laughing when he spoke.

"I guess I'd better get on your side of this argument, Del. I know what you're up against. I've been through it all myself. And people wouldn't believe me either."

They parked and went into the airport to wait for the plane.

CHAPTER 2

A POLICE SEARCH

It had been decided that Kay and the triplets and their cousins would spend at least part of the month's vacation with Danny's parents at Angle Inlet. Danny had a lot of flying to do and would be away most of the time, and Kay thought that would be a good opportunity to visit his parents.

Danny planned to take Kay and DeeDee and Marie to the Northwest Angle of Minnesota in one trip and the boys in another. However, the night after they got back from Minneapolis with Phil and Marie, he had an emergency call to the Yukon, Canada, and had to leave the following morning.

"I don't like this, Kay, because it's going to make a long bus ride for all of you, but there doesn't seem to be any choice. I can't delay the mission trip."

Kay took Danny out to the airport and rushed back to get the kids ready for the trip to Warroad by bus. Del and Doug had made arrangements with one of the neighbors to keep their riding horses while they were gone. Jumper, of course, was running free and wouldn't need anyone to look after him. As for his crow, Blackie, Del planned on taking him along.

Kay questioned the wisdom of that decision. "As far as I'm concerned, I don't care if you take him, Del. But do you think the driver will let him on the bus?"

Determination glinted in the boy's eyes. "I don't know why they wouldn't. I'll take him in his cage. He can't hurt anything." The boy straightened. "If I can't take him with me, I just won't go. That's all there is to it."

Kay smiled reassuringly. "We'll have to see what the situation is."

When they came to get on the bus, the driver eyed Blackie critically.

"And where do you think you're going, young man?" he asked Del.

The boy tightened the grip on the cage. He knew what the driver meant, but he pretended not to.

"To Warroad, why?"

"That's not what I'm talking about. "What're you doing with that crow?"

The boy's eyes brightened.

"This is a genuine trained talking crow," he informed him proudly. "He goes with me wherever I go."

The driver squinted at him doubtfully.

"You don't expect me to believe that, now do you?"

"It's the truth."

"If he's a talking crow, what does he say?"

As though on cue, Blackie cocked his head.

"Hello. Hello. Blackie is a good crow. Blackie is a good crow."

The driver gasped, and disbelief crept into his eyes.

"You ain't one of them ventriloquists, are you?"

"Not on your life," Del retorted. "That was Blackie talking. Didn't you see him?"

The driver scratched his head.

"I've hauled a lot of funny things on buses in my time, but this is the first time I ever hauled a crow that could talk!"

"Is–is it all right if I take him with me?"

The driver grinned. "I don't think there're any regulations against taking a talking crow to your seat with you as long as you keep him in that cage, so he doesn't fly around and scare the passengers or get into my hair."

Del assured him that Blackie was a perfect gentleman, probably as well-mannered and polite as any passenger he had ever hauled.

"Even if he was out of his cage, he wouldn't fly around. He'd stay right with me all the time. He's the best trained crow in all of Minnesota."

Doug and Phil, who had been standing behind Del listening to the interchange of talk, grinned broadly as Del led the way to a seat halfway back, proudly carrying Blackie in his cage. He was quite conscious of the fact that everyone on the bus was looking at him and his crow. Phil eyed the bird with growing wonder.

"I didn't think you could get him to do it," he said quietly when they were seated. "I figured you were kidding when you told me that you'd taught your crow to talk."

Del's voice crescendoed triumphantly. "You heard him, didn't you?" he exclaimed. "You know now that he can talk if he wants to."

Phil's eyes brightened with pride.

"I sure wish I had a trained crow to take back to the ranch with us when we go. Do you suppose we could catch another one while we're up here and teach him to talk too?"

Del considered that briefly. He didn't know whether they could or not. It was a lot of work catching a crow in the first place and even harder to teach him to talk. Besides, he didn't know if he wanted anyone else – even his cousin – to have another talking crow. He sort of liked the idea of having the only one he knew about.

"It would be rough to do."

Phil grinned. "Wouldn't Dad's eyes bug out if I came home with a crow that we'd taught to speak. He wouldn't believe it even if he heard him. No sir, he just wouldn't believe it."

Doug, who was sitting on the seat behind them, leaned forward enough to hear what was being said.

"That's right. I've been living around this stupid crow for months, and I still don't believe it!" He tried to joke, but there was a bite to his words.

The corners of Del's mouth firmed.

"I don't know why you wouldn't believe it," he countered. "You've heard him talk. You know he can do it."

"Maybe it's like the driver said. Maybe you're learning ventriloquism."

Del snorted his indignation.

"I know what's wrong with you. You're just jealous because Blackie belongs to me, that's all. You'd like to have him all to yourself."

"You mean to tell me that I'd like to have a stupid crow?" His face wrinkled distastefully. "You must be out of your ever-lovin' mind."

Del settled back in the seat, irritation sealing his lips. It was a long while before he spoke again. The trouble with that brother of his was that he couldn't stand to have Del get ahead of him, even with a pet like Blackie. He wouldn't have spent the time to have caught the crow, let alone tame him and work with him until he finally learned to speak. He was too crazy about basketball and football.

Doug had to be in the limelight. He couldn't stand it if people didn't pay attention to him. Briefly, jealousy stung Del's heart.

Doug's frown deepened. He had only been kidding Del. He didn't know why he had to get his back up like a fighting cock. He was getting so touchy that Doug couldn't kid him at all without making him mad.

It was late that night when the bus pulled into Warroad, Minnesota. Kay and the kids were about to go into the hotel where they would spend the night when Marie stopped and turned to Del.

"What are you going to do with Blackie tonight?" she asked.

"What do you think? I'm going to take him up to our room."

"Will they let you?" she persisted.

"They let me take him on the bus, didn't they?"

Nevertheless, Marie's doubts bothered Del. The clerk just might get touchy if he happened to see Blackie. If he didn't let him keep the crow in his room, he'd have to go somewhere else with him. But where? That was a question that troubled him.

When they went into the hotel lobby, he stood some distance from the desk, holding the cage as casually at his side as though every second or third guest carried a tame crow. He even turned his body slightly to further screen the cage from the sleepy night clerk. But it didn't seem to make any difference. Either that, or the clerk didn't notice the cage. He said nothing about it as he showed them up to their room.

Del turned to Marie when the clerk went back downstairs.

"Well," he said triumphantly, "I did it, didn't I?"

Sheer admiration glinted in her eyes.

"I didn't know I had such a smart cousin."

Doug laughed. "He's smart, all right. He plays with a crow when he could go out for football or basketball."

Del cringed and his cheeks flushed. He would have said something to that disgusting brother of his, but at that moment Kay told them they had better get to their own rooms and get ready for bed.

"We've got to get up early in the morning to have breakfast and get down to the dock in time to catch the *Island Queen,*" she said.

In spite of the fact that they were all exhausted from their long bus ride, they were up at 6:00 the next morning, had breakfast, and were down to the dock by 7:30. Cap and his helper had just arrived and were getting ready to make the trip. They both recognized Kay and were glad to see her.

"It looks as though you're going to be the only passengers on the run today," the captain of the *Island Queen* told them.

The boys helped put the freight aboard the little packet boat. No other passengers showed up, and at 8:00 they were ready to shove off for the run across the Big Traverse to Flag and Oak islands and Angle Inlet when a state patrol car came driving up, siren screaming. Del looked out and saw the officers get out hurriedly.

"Who do you suppose they're after?" he murmured curiously.

Doug glanced in his brother's direction.

"Maybe they're after that stupid crow of yours. Maybe the hotel found out you had him in our room and is going to press charges."

Del colored. "They may be after Blackie, but they're not going to get him. I'll guarantee you that much right now."

The patrolmen called Cap to one side and talked with him in low tones. Then the taller of the two officers stepped aboard the *Island Queen*. He opened the door and looked around.

"I don't want to frighten any of you," the officer said, "but we're going to have to take a look around the *Island Queen* before you leave."

With that the two officers began to search the boat thoroughly.

CHAPTER 3

TROUBLE AT ANGLE INLET?

Cap sat stiffly at the wheel of the *Island Queen* and waited while the state police officers made their search. They opened the front compartment where Cap and his mate slept when they laid over at Angle Inlet twice a week. Satisfied that the compartment in the bow was empty, they went back to the fantail. As they shoved past the Davis boys and Phil, one of the officers spoke softly to the other.

"I think this is a waste of time."

"So do I, but we've got to do it. Orders are orders." Del shifted Blackie's cage from one knee to the other and turned to stare after the police officers. Blackie cocked his head saucily and opened one eye, as though he was the wisest bird around.

"Hello."

The uniformed men spun about.

"Who said that?" one of them demanded.

Before Del had an opportunity to say anything, Blackie continued. "Hello, Barney. Hello, Barney."

"My name's not Barney!" The officer's voice rose. "Who said that?"

Del's eyes widened.

"Shh, you dumb crow!" he whispered tensely.

Phil snickered.

The officer came storming back to where Del was sitting.

"What's going on here?" He was cold and demanding. "Are you making fun of us?"

Del struggled for words. "I–I–" He knew that his face was crimson, but he couldn't help that. If that dumb Blackie had just kept still, everything would have been all right. But no! He had to spout off. And now he was in for it. He'd probably lose Blackie and be in trouble besides.

But the crow didn't seem to care about the trouble he was causing. He kept right on talking.

"Hello. Hello, Barney," he repeated. "Hello, Barney."

The officer stared.

"Is this really happening?" he asked. "Or am I seeing things?"

Blackie seemed aware of the fact that he had an audience. His eyes gleamed, and there was a saucy note in his voice.

"Run, Doug, run! Hello, Del. Hello, Barney. Hello. Hello."

The other police officer came back and stood beside his partner, who was pointing at the crow.

"Do you see what I see, Johnny?"

"I don't know what you see, but I'm looking at a crow."

"It's a crow all right, but it's the strangest crow I ever saw. He talks."

The officer turned to Del.

Del nodded miserably. Now he was in big trouble. He'd never be able to talk his way out of this mess.

Then the police officer grinned.

"Tell me something. Where did you get a talking crow, anyway?"

Del grinned his relief. They weren't going to do anything about Blackie. They were just curious because they had never seen a talking crow before.

"I caught him and taught him to talk. I mean an Indian friend and I taught him to talk. Don't you think he does pretty good?"

"Pretty good? He beats Johnny, here."

"Come off it, will you," the one called Johnny said good-naturedly.

For half a minute they stared at the boy and his pet, disbelief glittering in their eyes.

"Make him talk again."

Del tried. How he tried. He said everything Blackie had ever said and some of the new words he and Barney had been working on.

"Hello, Barney." As a last resort he fell back on

that phrase. It was the one the crow said most frequently. "Hello, Barney. Hello."

But Blackie had quit talking, and it was useless trying to make him say anything else. He eyed Del impishly and kept his beak shut. The two policemen shook their heads.

"If we hadn't heard him ourselves, I don't believe I would have ever believed it."

"I still don't believe it," his companion said, "and I saw him open his beak and heard the words come out."

One of the men looked at his watch.

"We've got to get moving." He turned to Cap. "Keep your eyes open, and if you see anything unusual, let us know right away."

"I'll do that."

"Fine."

The two men stepped ashore. The mate loosed the line, gave the *Island Queen* a shove out into the current, and stepped aboard as the little packet boat edged away. Phil turned to Del.

"I thought you were going to be in real trouble for a couple of minutes there when old Blackie started to talk." He snickered. "Those two cops were sure fooled, weren't they?"

"You can say that again." Del shrugged. "But there wasn't anything to get upset about. There wasn't anything they could do. There's no law against a crow talking."

"I guess not," Phil said, chuckling, "but I sure got scared for a minute."

Doug, who had been looking at the houses along the riverbank, turned to Del and Phil.

"What do you suppose they were trying to find, anyway?" he asked.

Phil replied in guarded tones. "I don't know, but they sure did give the *Island Queen* a going over. They must have figured that whatever they were looking for was on board."

Del started to speak, but he saw that DeeDee and Marie were listening to their conversation intently, so he checked himself. There was no need in getting them all excited. They'd be so scared they wouldn't leave the house when they got up to Uncle Carl's.

Deep inside, Del knew that wasn't true, but it made him feel a little braver himself to think about how frightened the girls would be.

"Come on," he said, getting to his feet and setting Blackie's cage on the seat where he had been sitting. "Let's go to the back of the boat where we can talk without some people overhearing us."

DeeDee wrinkled her nose at him.

Moving the crow was enough to set him to chattering once more.

"Hello, Barney," he called, sounding almost exactly like Del. "Hello, Barney. Hello. Hello."

Del laughed. "Isn't that just like that stupid Blackie.

When we wanted him to talk, he wouldn't say a word, but just listen to him now. He's talking all the time."

But Doug and Phil weren't even listening to him. They were too concerned about the police officers and their search of the *Island Queen* a few minutes before. They made their way to the fantail of the boat and huddled together.

"Why'd you want to come out here, Del?" Doug asked.

"I just wanted to talk to you about those two patrolmen, and I was afraid that if we did it inside where DeeDee and Marie were listening to us, they'd soon know everything that we know."

Their cousin Phil broke in quickly.

"But we don't know anything. That's the rub."

Del breathed deeply. "We know the police are looking for something or someone." He paused and glanced about as though there was danger of being overheard even from where they were. "We know that much at least."

Phil nodded. That wasn't much to know, but it was a starting place.

"And we know that Cap knows what it's all about," Del continued. "That's something else."

"But he's not going to tell us," Doug put in. "I'll guarantee you that."

"Maybe not, but it's not going to hurt to try."

Doug and Phil turned that over in their minds. What Del said was true. Cap had to know what the authorities were looking for. There just might be a possibility that he would tell them something that might give them an idea as to what was going on.

"Who's going to talk to him?" Doug asked.

"I will, if you guys will go in and talk to the girls so they don't hear everything that's said."

Doug and Phil went into the cabin and started talking with the girls about the lake and the fun they were going to have at Uncle Carl's. When the conversation was going well, Del came in and went forward to the place where Cap was standing, his hand on the wheel.

At first he said nothing but looked out across the wide expanse of the Big Traverse that lay flat and motionless as a mirror before them. He asked Cap a question or two about navigating on the big lake and how they were able to stay on course. The gray-haired skipper seemed to like to talk and answered his questions even more fully than he expected, with a few stories about his earlier days on the lake thrown in. When Del felt that he had gotten well enough acquainted with the captain of the *Island Queen,* he approached the subject that had brought him to the front of the cabin to talk with Cap in the first place.

"I was sure scared when those police came charging in and looked around before we left," he said.

There was no answer.

Del swallowed hard and tried again.

"Do they come around like this very often?"

Cap shook his head. "Nope. As a matter of fact, I can't say that it's ever happened to me before. Leastwise, if it has, I can't remember it."

Del eyed him obliquely.

"It sure makes a guy wonder what they were looking for."

"I reckon it does." He squinted at the compass and corrected their heading by two degrees. It was a minute or more before he answered. "But it doesn't matter. They didn't find what they were after."

Del waited a moment and tried again on another tack, but he was no more successful than he had been the first time. At last, in desperation, he gave up and went back to his seat. DeeDee eyed him knowingly.

"What's the matter? Wouldn't he tell you what the patrolmen were looking for when they came aboard a little while ago?"

The muscles in Del's mouth tightened. That DeeDee! She thought she was so smart! Let her try to get any information out of Cap and she'd find out that it wasn't so easy. He wasn't about to tell anybody anything.

When the three boys went to the back of the boat again, Doug and Phil were excited to learn what Del had found out about the police officers and why they had searched the *Island Queen*.

"What did Cap tell you?" Doug whispered.

"Not a thing. Not a single thing!"

"I'm not surprised," Phil put in. "I didn't expect him to tell you anything."

Del was silent for a while.

"But, you know, the way I figure, it has something to do with the Angle."

"What makes you say that?"

"The *Island Queen* goes out to the Angle, doesn't she? And the cops came just before we left."

"She stops other places too," Doug reminded him.

"Maybe. But I still think it has something to do with Uncle Carl's."

CHAPTER 4

ARRIVAL OF MYSTERIOUS VISITORS

As the *Island Queen* approached Angle Inlet, Kay got to her feet, her excitement growing. Then she walked back to the fantail and stood beside the boys, trying to make out the identity of the figures on the Orlis dock. DeeDee and Marie crowded in beside her.

"Can you see Uncle Carl and Aunt Mary?" DeeDee asked, almost as excited as Kay.

At that moment the figures on the dock began to wave vigorously.

"I can now!" Kay was waving in return.

As the little packet boat glided expertly toward the dock, the Davis boys and Phil pushed up against the railing. They were off the *Island Queen* as soon as the mate secured the lines. For several minutes everybody was laughing and talking at the same time. The boys were shouting questions about the fishing, and Carl and Mary Orlis were trying to find out how everybody had been and how long Danny would be away.

At last the noise began to quiet down. Carl glanced at his watch.

"I think it's about time we go in the house and see if we can get something to eat, don't you?" he asked.

Mrs. Orlis beamed. "And you'll never guess what I've got in the oven."

Doug spoke up quickly. "A cake!"

"That's right! You sound just like Danny. When he was your age, he was always after me to bake a chocolate cake, and that was what he usually guessed was in the oven."

They walked up to the house together. As they did so, Phil asked the question that had been on his mind ever since he learned that they were going to be spending much of the summer at the Angle.

"How's the fishing, Mr. Orlis?"

Carl put a hand on the boy's shoulder.

"It just so happens that it's pretty good right now," he said. "In fact, it's the best that it's been for a couple of years."

Phil's eyes lit up.

"Hey, Del, did you hear that? The fishing's good."

Del spoke up. "What did I tell you? The fishing's always good here."

"I can hardly wait to get out and give it a whirl."

"You won't have to wait long. You can go out and start fishing the first thing in the morning."

They were in the house before Carl noticed the crow that Del was carrying in the cage.

"So, this is Blackie that we've been hearing so much about."

"That's right." The boy's eyes brightened. "Only, don't expect him to say anything. Whenever I want him to talk, he won't do it, and when I want him to keep still, he talks a streak."

Carl laughed. "He sounds just like the Blackie we used to have when Danny was a boy." He sat down in the living room and leaned back in the chair. "We sure used to have a lot of fun with him around here."

Carl continued to remember some of the things that Danny's pet crow had done. Del scooted forward, as though he feared missing a word. Doug and Phil were as interested as he was, only it wasn't quite so apparent.

* * *

The following morning the three boys borrowed a boat from Mr. Orlis and filled the tank with the gas and oil mixture that outboards use. Kay came down to the dock as they were stowing their tackle aboard, concern clouding her face.

"Dad, do you think it's all right for the boys to go out on the lake alone?" she asked.

Carl looked up, eyes twinkling.

"That husband of yours was roaming all over this lake when he was little more than half as old as these guys."

"But Danny was born and raised here. He knew the lake."

"They know exactly where they can go and where they can't, and they'll be wearing life jackets. You don't have to worry about them. They'll take care of themselves."

Kay's smile flashed.

"I know they will, Dad. I shouldn't get so concerned about them. You wouldn't let them go out on the lake if it wasn't safe."

The boys shoved off and started the engine.

Mr. Orlis had told them they could fish around the islands a quarter of a mile or so out from the mouth of Pine Creek. There was a weed bed on the east end of the near island that he had suggested they try first. They hadn't trolled more than a hundred yards before Phil caught a plump walleye.

Doug, who had cast toward shore while they were waiting for Phil to get his fish on the stringer, squealed with delight. He had one too, a slim, fighting northern pike that arced his rod double. In less than two minutes they had two fish in the boat.

"And just this morning I was thinking that I wished Danny was here to tell us where to find the fish."

They caught several more fish the first hour, not

counting those they weren't able to land. Phil could talk of little else.

"I didn't think there were any places like this to fish," he said. "I sure would like to have Dad up here. He likes to fish even better than I do."

Del had fallen silent. There was a faraway look in his eyes, and he scarcely heard what the other two were saying. He liked to fish too, but this particular morning he couldn't get interested in it. At last he spoke.

"I don't know about you guys, but I still can't help thinking about those cops. I sure would like to know what they were looking for when they searched the *Island Queen* yesterday morning."

Doug nodded. "So would I. Do you suppose they found what they were after?"

Del changed lures and dropped the red and white metal wobbler over the side of the boat into the water.

"I wish there was some way of finding out what that was all about," he said.

"We'd just as well forget that. We tried to get some information out of Cap, but he wouldn't tell us anything."

"I suppose you're right." Del sighed his disappointment once more. "But it sounded so mysterious."

When they got back to the dock shortly before noon, Carl was waiting for them.

"Now you've done the easy part," he said, watching while they tied the boat securely.

They looked up.

"What do you mean?"

"You've caught the fish. Now, if you'll come over to the shed, I'll show you how to fillet them."

Doug groaned in mock dismay.

"You mean we've got to clean our own fish after we've gone to all the work of catching them?"

"Around here, anyone who catches fish cleans them," Carl informed him.

Carl showed them how to fillet the fish and went into the house with them. Mary, Kay, and the girls were sitting around the table.

"What's going on in here, anyway?" Carl asked, looking from one to the other and speaking with a reproach he did not feel. "We thought you'd be fixing something to eat."

Mary glanced up at them.

"We were just listening to the news from Warroad," she said. "There have been two more robberies down there."

Carl's eyes narrowed.

"Didn't they catch the thieves yet?"

His wife shook her head.

"Not yet. The news says they have very little evidence to go on."

Del glanced quickly at Phil and his brother. That must have been what the police came aboard the *Island Queen* the day before to check out. Maybe they thought some of the stolen goods were aboard the little packet boat!

$* * *$

That night the boys made sure that they got to hear the late evening news again before they went to bed. However, it was only a repeat of the earlier broadcast. There was no new information.

"Well, they sure didn't tell us anything we didn't already know," Phil said disgustedly. "We'd just as well have gone to bed an hour ago."

"We could have told you that much," Marie answered. "But you didn't ask us. You have to make a big secret of everything."

The boys did not answer her. It was not long, though, before they went into the bedroom that the three of them were sharing during their stay at Angle Inlet. As soon as the door was shut, they huddled together, talking in furtive whispers.

"Those stupid girls! They think they've got to be in on everything we do or even talk about."

Del nodded. "They aren't going to find out anything from us."

"We might have to find out some things from them," Doug added.

They looked at one another.

"I still wonder why the police were checking the *Island Queen*," Phil said. "Cap isn't in on anything that isn't honest, I'd bet on that. And nobody else would hide anything on board."

"You mean you don't think anyone else would hide anything on board," Del said. "Maybe the guy who helps Cap is in on it."

"Not a chance," Doug countered. "I heard Uncle Carl say that he's known Kenny Stearns since he was a little kid and that he's all right."

"And that," Phil added, "leaves us right back where we started from."

* * *

The following morning Carl had a radio message from Warroad. He came into the kitchen where his wife and Kay and the kids were having breakfast.

"Well, Mary, it looks as though we're going to have some company."

She looked up. "Fishermen?"

"Nope. At least I don't imagine that she'll be doing much fishing." He handed the piece of paper to his wife.

"Read this."

She read aloud. "Reserve cabin for one for three weeks. Arriving *Island Queen* today. Mrs. Edith Braisted."

The little group eyed one another curiously.

"Doesn't it seem strange to you that a woman

would come out to a place like this alone to spend the summer?" Kay asked of no one in particular.

* * *

Del, Doug, and Phil went down to the dock and cleaned up a couple of boats for Mr. Orlis. Then they filled the tanks with gas and checked the plugs on the outboard motors. Del, who had been thinking about his pet crow, stopped suddenly.

"Know what I'm going to do?" he asked. "As soon as we get through here, I'm going to let Blackie loose and see what happens."

Doug spoke quickly. "Do you think you dare?"

"Uncle Carl said he thought it would be all right, and he ought to know."

They went to the barn where Del had been keeping Blackie at night and got the cage with the bird in it.

"OK, old fellow. We're going to let you out of that cage now."

The crow eyed him impishly. "Hello, Barney. Hello, Barney. Hello. Hello."

Phil laughed. "What a stupid crow. He doesn't even know you from Barney."

"Stupid crow. Stupid crow!" Blackie repeated. "Hello, Barney. Hello."

"He's not so stupid," Del said defensively. "He's just an individualist."

Doug snorted.

That seemed to upset Del. He stopped uncertainly, staring at his pet.

"Stupid crow. Stupid crow."

Del loosened the latch on the cage, and the door swung open. He had thought the crow would dart out immediately, but instead, Blackie remained motionless, blinking as though he couldn't quite make out what was happening.

"Come on, Blackie. You don't have to stay in that old cage any longer. Come on out." He reached in gently and took the bird in his hand. Blackie struggled a bit, but as soon as the boy got him out of the cage, he relaxed his grip. The crow looked around and, lifting his wings, flew to the edge of the barn roof. Perched there, he lifted his voice to the trees.

"Run, Doug! Run!"

Del talked to him for several moments. Blackie remained on the roof for a time but, tiring of that, he soared down to a stump almost at Del's feet.

"Hello, Del. Hello. Hello."

Doug grinned. "He is going to stick around, after all."

They were still fooling around with Blackie when the whine of a large outboard motor broke the silence.

Phil spun to stare up the creek at the bay where the sound was coming from.

"It sounds as though that Mrs. Braisted is going to get here before Uncle Carl expected her."

"That's not her." Doug's voice was scoffing. "She

said she was going to be coming on the *Island Queen* and she won't be getting in here until four o'clock this afternoon."

Del nodded. "Well, whoever it is, he's sure in an awful hurry," he acknowledged.

The boys left the barn and made their way down to the dock. They hadn't had time to get out on the heavy wooden pier before a large white fiberglass cruiser banked into the creek and roared in the direction of the dock.

Phil gasped. "Look at 'em come!" Awe tinged his youthful voice.

An Indian boy who was standing beside the man at the wheel suddenly thrust a brown arm into the air, waving vigorously.

Del, who saw how fast they were coming, stooped to fend off the boat from the pilings as she glided in.

"Hi," Doug said. But nobody returned his greeting.

"Is this Carl Orlis's place?" The speaker straightened at the wheel, revealing a lank, spindly torso. Bronzed skin hung loosely over his cheekbones, accentuating the hollows below his blue eyes.

"That's right."

Startled at the voice from the porch, Del spun quickly. Carl must have heard the newcomers too. He had left the house and spoke as he approached the dock at a leisurely gait.

"I'm Carl Orlis."

The men got out and secured their boat to the

dock. The boys were eyeing the strangers quizzically, but Carl seemed to have no questions about them. He waited patiently until they were ready to continue the conversation. At last, they directed their attention to him.

"My name's Ralph White and this is Charlie Wilson, Mr. Orlis. We were told in Warroad that if we wanted to get some walleyes and big northerns we ought to come up and stay with you."

Charlie broke in. "Got any room for us?"

Carl nodded. "There's a cabin you can rent."

The one who said his name was Ralph glanced at the Indian boy who had guided them out to the Angle.

"Get our gear, boy. We want to move in and get out on the bay to try our luck fishing."

He walked off the dock, and his companion, Charlie, followed. Carl glanced at the boys, but they had already anticipated the request to help the Indian lad who had just come, and they had gotten into the boat to help carry some of the gear.

The newcomer stared at them.

"I can get it."

"Sure, you can. But there's no use in your carrying everything when we don't have anything to do," Del told him.

As they helped the boy get the men's gear over to the cabin where they would be staying, they learned that his name was Marcel. Even though they helped, they didn't get the bags to the cabin fast enough to suit the fishermen.

"Snap it up, Marcel." Charlie's voice wore a thin, grating edge. "We want to get out there and see what those fish are doing."

Doug and Del said little until after the men in their fancy boat had roared away to the fishing grounds Mr. Orlis had told them about.

"I don't think I'd like to be in Marcel's shoes."

"Neither would I," Phil said, keeping his voice down. "Why do you suppose he came with them anyway?"

"I don't know. I just figured he was their guide."

Del thought about that momentarily. "Could be, but I don't see how he could do much guiding around here. The way he acted, I don't think he's ever been here before. He doesn't seem to know anything about fishing on this part of the lake."

Doug nodded in agreement. "Anyway, he's sure going to earn whatever they're paying him. I can tell you that much."

CHAPTER 5

ANOTHER MYSTERIOUS VISITOR

DeeDee and Marie didn't get to see the men who had arrived at Angle Inlet unexpectedly that morning. They had come roaring in, rented a cabin, and went roaring out to fish so quickly that the girls were scarcely aware that anyone had come at all until they were gone again. They tried to find out from their brothers why the men had come to Uncle Carl's.

"They just came to fish," Del said mysteriously. "Why else would a couple of fishermen come to a fishing camp?"

"You've been whispering around all morning," Marie reminded him. "What is it? Why are you so interested in them if they're just a couple of fishermen?"

A smile crept into Del's eyes, and he winked at Phil and Doug.

"You wouldn't be interested. You're just girls."

"Oh, wouldn't we?" DeeDee's anger flashed. "You don't need to think you're so smart. We'll find out what this is all about."

"When you do," Doug added, "let us know."

"We will not!" She stamped her foot. "When we find out, we won't tell you a single thing."

At last the boys tired of teasing their sisters and sauntered off.

"I get *so* mad at them!" DeeDee stormed. "We'll find out what those men came for. And when we do, we're not going to say anything to the boys either. We'll show them!"

"Maybe they were telling us all they know," Marie said. "Maybe those men are just fishermen."

DeeDee shook her head.

"There's got to be some other reason they came up here. I know Doug and Del. They wouldn't be so excited about them if they didn't think there was something strange going on."

Marie thought about that. She didn't know for sure if DeeDee was right, but if she was, Marie wanted to get things unraveled before her cousins and Phil did. She didn't like the way those boys acted as though they knew everything just because they were boys.

They talked about various ways of finding out what the men were doing at Uncle Carl's, and finally decided that there was nothing they could do about it until the strangers got back. Then, maybe they could get to talking to them or to the Indian boy who had come along with them or something.

Although the girls said nothing about the men where the boys could overhear them, they kept a close watch for the white boat that morning. They were surprised when the men didn't even come in for lunch at noon. After helping with the dishes, the girls went for a walk along the creek and then for a swim. They were just changing back into their clothes when the *Island Queen* pulled in. Marie flew to the window and parted the curtain.

"Cap's here!" she exclaimed. "And I see a woman on board. It must be that Mrs. Braisted!"

DeeDee moved quickly to the window beside her cousin. The two girls watched motionlessly while Cap's helper hopped nimbly to the dock and snubbed the *Island Queen* close. The boys and Uncle Carl were there to give him a hand if he needed it, but there was nothing for them to do. The boy on the *Island Queen* was adept at his job.

Marie glanced quickly at DeeDee.

"Do you see Mrs. Braisted?" she asked.

DeeDee hesitated. When Marie first spoke as the *Island Queen* began to move in to the dock, she thought she had seen their new guest. Now she wondered if she had seen anyone at all.

"I don't see anyone, do you?"

"Not now," Marie said. "I–"

"There's Cap!" Triumph tinged DeeDee's voice.

"And there's someone else beside him. That must be Mrs. Braisted!"

A spare, wide-shouldered woman, with efficiency indelibly stamped in every move, climbed out of the packet boat and turned to Carl Orlis.

"Are you Mr. Orlis?" she demanded, her voice sharp and strident. DeeDee and Marie could hear her plainly, although they were inside and some distance away.

"That's right," Uncle Carl told her genially, thrusting out his hand. "And you must be Mrs. Braisted."

She looked him over coolly.

"Well, don't just stand there. Get my bags and show me to my cabin. I've had a tiring trip on that miserable little boat."

Carl eyed her deliberately, an amused smile toying with the corners of his mouth. He acted as though he was about to speak but changed his mind.

"Would you boys help with this luggage?" he asked calmly.

"Sure thing," Doug spoke up quickly. "You go ahead with Mrs. Braisted. We'll take her stuff to the cabin."

The woman scowled uneasily.

"Do you trust these boys to handle the luggage of your guests, Mr. Orlis?"

"Of course."

Still, she wasn't satisfied. She turned back to the

boys. "You won't drop my bags and break anything, will you?"

"No, ma'am," Phil said as respectfully as he could under the circumstances. "We'll be careful."

Doug could not resist. "We haven't broken a pair of pajamas or a sweater for a coon's age."

Edith Braisted snorted indignantly.

"Smart! Is that any way for you to talk to your elders?"

Doug, realizing how his remark must have sounded, apologized.

"I'm sorry. I was just trying to make a little joke."

"Well, it wasn't very humorous, I can assure you." She paused for a moment. "I have some most fragile valuables in my bags, and I wouldn't be at all happy if they were broken."

Carl started to intervene, but the boys were picking up Mrs. Braisted's luggage. At least they picked up as much of it as they could and left the dock. They made three trips before they had everything in the little cabin.

"Whew!" Del mopped his forehead with his sweating hand. "I thought we never were going to get all of that gear hauled into her cabin. You know, there's not going to be much room for her in there with all those suitcases and boxes."

"She sure has a lot of junk," Doug said, sitting down and leaning against a tree. "Why do you suppose anyone would bring so much gear to a place like this?"

There was a moment's silence.

"She's going to stay for three weeks."

"Yeah, I know that. But she's got enough stuff for two years."

Blackie, who must have been watching them, flew down to a spot a yard or so from Del.

"Hello, Barney," he said.

"That isn't Barney, Stupid," Doug said. "That's Del."

"Hello, Barney! Hello, Barney!" As he repeated the phrase, the crow hopped about excitedly, stopping every now and then to focus beady eyes on his youthful master.

Del held out his hand and the crow hopped over to him.

"You're lucky you're a crow. You didn't have to help carry all of Mrs. Braisted's gear."

Doug saw Carl head for the post office in the shed behind the barn, a small sack of mail in his hand. He jumped to his feet.

"Oh boy!" he exclaimed. "Mail!"

DeeDee had also seen Carl start for the post office with the incoming mail.

"Come on, Marie." She opened the bedroom door. "Let's go and see if Uncle Carl has any mail for us."

Marie's dark eyes gleamed.

"Maybe Phil and I will have a letter from Mom and Dad."

DeeDee jerked her head to focus quickly on her cousin. It had been months since she had been deeply upset by the death of her parents, but for some reason, Marie's casual reference to her own parents tore at DeeDee. No matter how she longed for a letter, she would never hear from her parents again. It didn't seem fair, somehow.

Grimly, DeeDee forced her thoughts to more pleasant things.

Carl was in no hurry to get the mail sorted. Quite deliberately he unlocked his heavy padlock on the canvas bag and dumped the mail onto the counter. Then, with painstaking slowness, he began to shuffle through the letters, two or three at a time.

There was a letter from Danny for Kay, two letters for Phil and Marie from their parents, and a letter from Fairview for DeeDee. She recognized the scented stationery and the handwriting.

Sandy Cole had written, after all! Her heart soared as she opened the envelope and began to read.

Everything was about the same at home, Sandy wrote. The gang went swimming almost every day. Wally Crowder had given another of his famous parties with all of the kids who were anybody at school invited. And he had asked Sandy about DeeDee and when she would be getting back.

Wally said the only thing wrong with the party was that you weren't there. He still thinks you're somebody very special. I think you're going to be seeing a lot of him next year.

The reference to Wally lighted DeeDee's young

face. He was somebody very special to her too. At that moment, homesickness all but overwhelmed her. It would be great to be back in Fairview with Sandy and Wally and their friends. They'd really have a blast.

Leaving the subject of the kids, Sandy went on to write about her parents.

I thought things were going to be wonderful when Dad promised to quit drinking. And for a while he didn't drink at all. Then he and Mom had an argument about something, and he went out and started drinking again. We didn't see or hear anything of him for three days.

DeeDee paused.

It must be terrible to live the way Sandy lives, she reasoned. She was so thankful that she and the boys had been born into a Christian home and now were being raised by Christians. She couldn't even imagine what it would be like to have drinking and bickering going on at home. But she knew from that awful night when Mr. Cole had come home drunk when she was staying with Sandy that it was worse than almost anything she could think of.

She continued to read her friend's letter.

The night Dad came home, he and Mom had such a terrible argument that I wanted to run away and never see either of them again. Danny and Kay might not let you do some of the things you'd like to, and they don't have nearly as much money as my parents have, but you don't know how I envy you, DeeDee. I'd give anything in the world if my parents were like Danny and Kay and would show how much they really love me by trying to make me do what's right.

DeeDee read that part of the letter over again thoughtfully. Strange, she had always envied Sandy for the big house she lived in and the closet full of clothes that she had and parents who didn't ask her where she had been or whom she had been with when she was out. Now she found that Sandy actually envied her. She folded the paper with care.

What Sandy had written was true, she realized. Danny and Kay loved her and the boys so much, and they were concerned about the way they would grow up and the things that they did. She had stormed around, trying to make herself believe they were old-fashioned and behind the times. But all the while she had known that was not true. Now Sandy wrote that she actually envied her for the consistent Christian home Danny and Kay provided.

DeeDee's somber manner brightened.

God had been very good in providing her and the boys with the sort of Christian home they were living in. She had never been more conscious of it than at that very moment. She was going to let Kay read the letter, she told herself, and tell her how thankful she was that they made her and her brothers mind and gave them a fine Christian testimony as an example to live up to.

CHAPTER 6

A SPECIAL LETTER

Ralph White and his companion came in from the lake shortly before six o'clock that evening. If they had caught any fish, they didn't say anything about it. The two men came into the Orlis living room and sat down to wait for dinner. Carl took a chair across from them.

"Did you have any luck fishing today?" he asked.

Ralph squinted at him glumly.

"It was all right, I guess," he said. "I've seen better fishing than we had today, but maybe we shouldn't complain."

"The boys will fillet them for you if you'd like," Carl went on. "And any time you want to eat fish, Mary will fix them for a meal."

"Oh, no," Charlie broke in quickly. "Marcel can clean our fish. Your boys won't have to."

"And we've decided that we want to take home

those we catch," Ralph said. "So I don't think we'll be eating any while we're here – at least for now."

That seemed strange to Del and Doug. Most guys wanted to have at least a few fish dinners while they were at the lake.

Aunt Mary came to the door at that moment.

"Isn't there an Indian boy with you?" she asked.

The two men looked at her. "You mean Marcel?" one of them wanted to know.

"I don't know what his name is, but we're about ready to eat supper and I wondered where he is."

"He was with us all day," Ralph told her, "but, toward evening, he got to talking about some relatives he had living around here. He didn't say how far it was or when he would be back, so I don't know when you can expect him."

Mrs. Orlis faced Del and Doug.

"He surely wouldn't go too far away, although I can't figure out who around here would be a relative of his. Would you boys go out and see if you can find him? He must be half starved after being out on the lake all day."

Charlie spoke up quickly. "There's no use in your going off to look for him. He took one of the boats and went to the islands to visit a couple of cousins."

Carl did not speak immediately, but when he did, there was a firm tone in his voice that had not been there before.

"It's all right this time," he said, "but from now

on, I want to know when my boats are leaving and where they are going before they are used."

Charlie's eyes glittered in anger. "He asked me, and I said I thought it would be all right."

"After this, I would like to know *before* they go out," Carl said mildly.

Mary came in again and called them to dinner. Mrs. Braisted wasn't there when the others were seated, but she came in as Carl was asking the blessing. She glanced about disapprovingly and went to the empty place on Carl's left.

He introduced her to Aunt Mary and Kay and the others at the table. She nodded curtly in reply to the introductions and sat down. Kay tried to engage her in conversation.

"Have you ever been in this part of the country before?"

"No." The older woman's voice was short and uncommunicative.

"Ever since we got your message yesterday, I've been curious about something. How did you come to choose our place to spend the summer?"

The question was simple enough, but it seemed to upset Mrs. Braisted.

"A–a friend told me about it."

"That's interesting. Is it someone we know?"

The color fled from the new guest's cheeks.

"I–I don't feel very well," she stammered. "If you

will excuse me–" She got to her feet and fled from the room.

Del, Doug, and Phil started after her curiously. This was something they hadn't expected. Everybody at the Orlis house was acting strangely that day.

The boys were still thinking about it when Carl got the Bible and had devotions. As soon as the Bible reading and prayer were over, they excused themselves and went outside. Carl followed them to the door.

"It's going to be dark soon, guys. Don't be gone long."

Doug assured him that they wouldn't. "We'll be back in a little while. We've just got some things that we want to do."

They didn't speak again until they were far enough away from the house to be sure that they would not be overheard. On the banks of the creek they stopped, glancing about at the deepening shadows.

Del spoke in a whisper. "Where do you suppose Marcel went anyway?"

Frowning, Phil shook his head. "I don't know, but it seems sort of stupid to me that he'd go out to the islands at night. It's quite a ways, isn't it?"

"It's at least twelve or fifteen miles. It'd take him a long time in a heavy boat with the size motor that he's got," Doug replied.

"That's what I figured," Phil continued. "I just can't see a guy taking all that time when he would only have a few minutes to visit."

"Maybe he figured that he'd have to guide his fishermen in the daytime and wouldn't be able to go and visit," Del said.

"That's another thing." Doug's voice was thoughtful. "A guide is supposed to know the lake he's on. Why would Marcel try to guide fishermen up here? He doesn't know this part of the Lake of the Woods. Uncle Carl had to tell Ralph and Charlie where to fish."

Phil tugged at the lobe of his ear with growing uneasiness. "That's what I've been wondering. And another thing, why would a couple of experienced fishermen hire a guide who doesn't know the lake? It doesn't make sense to me."

"There's something else that's got me puzzled," Del said, straightening to his full height. "Why did Marcel disappear about the time Cap got here with the *Island Queen?* Do you suppose he was afraid to let old Cap see him?"

Doug's lips firmed. "Now, that's something I hadn't thought of. But he was around until Cap came in to the dock. I saw him myself." His voice lowered noticeably, and his companions leaned closer to catch what he was going to say. "Do you suppose he was afraid to have Cap or Kenny Stearns see him?"

The other two thought about that for a moment or two.

"Why would he be afraid of Cap?"

Doug shrugged his shoulders.

"Maybe we're getting too suspicious," he said.

Del could not agree with that.

"No, sir. There's something strange about those two men and Marcel. I don't know what it is, but I don't think they're what they try to tell us they are."

Phil did not reply, but he could not help agreeing with Del. There was something strange about the Indian boy and his two fishermen.

* * *

DeeDee was much quieter than usual that night as she helped with the dishes. Kay was so busy talking to Mrs. Orlis that she didn't notice, but Marie was curious about the change that had come over her cousin. As soon as the girls were alone in their room, she asked about it.

"No, there's nothing wrong with me." Her smile was thin and fleeting. "At least there's nothing wrong with me, personally. It–it's–"

"Was it the letter that you got this afternoon that's bothering you?" Marie asked.

DeeDee stared quickly at her, amazed at her perception.

"What makes you think the letter has anything to do with–with the fact that I haven't talked much tonight?"

Marie shrugged. "I don't know for sure, but you've acted awfully funny since you got that letter from your friend. So I figured that must have something to do with it."

DeeDee went over to the bench in front of the dresser and sat down on one corner of it.

"That letter from Sandy did have some bad news in it," she said, pausing uneasily. She didn't know whether she ought to go on or not, but she had started. She would have to tell Marie something. "Sandy's got a real problem at home."

DeeDee knew Sandy wouldn't want the people at Fairview to know about her parents. She had confided in DeeDee because she could trust her not to say anything about it. Then DeeDee realized that Marie would only be in Fairview a couple of days on their way home, and she wouldn't be likely to tell anyone, especially if she was warned not to. Nevertheless, DeeDee swore her cousin to secrecy before she read the letter to her.

Concern glittered in Marie's eyes.

"It must be terrible to have to live with that kind of trouble." There was a brief hesitation. "I know what it was like around our place when Dad got so mad at Phil when he–he got so 'religious.' And it was a lot worse when Mom did the same thing. The only one in the house he would talk to was me. I know just what Sandy is going through."

Marie fell silent. She had thought her dad would *never* get as religious as Mom and Phil, but he had. It made her sort of mad just to think about it. Earlier he had made her promise that she would never go overboard about the church the way they had, but now he was worse than any of them. But that didn't make any difference to her. She wasn't going to do that just because the rest of them had. She liked things the way they used to be. She wasn't *ever* going to change.

Once DeeDee had begun talking to her cousin, she was glad to have a chance to go over the whole affair with her.

"It's awfully hard for Sandy," she said. "She thinks her dad is going to quit drinking and that everything is going to be all right. It is all right for a little while, but the next thing she knows, he's at it again." She paused thoughtfully. "And she lives in such a beautiful home. It's one of those places you read about in magazines. I don't think I've ever been in any other house that's even half so beautiful."

Marie's frown deepened. "It doesn't sound so beautiful to me," she said. "It sounds ugly."

DeeDee squinted at her, disapproval written on her young face.

"You know what I mean."

She was greatly disturbed by Marie's attitude. It wasn't what her cousin said, exactly, as much as it was the tone of her voice. Marie sounded so much like Sandy in the letter that it bothered DeeDee. She picked up the letter once more and read it over silently. She would have to remember to pray for Sandy and her parents. Everyone had been so busy since they got to the Angle that she hadn't even thought about that.

Marie was silent for a time, her face twisting as though she was about to say more, but she was undecided as to whether she should or not. Then, abruptly, her expression changed.

"What made Mrs. Braisted act so funny at the table tonight?" she asked.

DeeDee eyed her curiously. At first she didn't remember what Marie was talking about. Then she recalled how disturbed their new guest had become at being questioned by Kay and how quickly she excused herself and left the table.

"I hadn't thought about that until right now. She did act strange, didn't she?"

"I don't think I've ever seen anyone get so upset because she was asked a few simple questions. It makes me wonder if she has something to hide."

* * *

DeeDee forgot about Mrs. Braisted when she went to her room that night. She started to undress for bed, but stopped and wrote a letter instead.

Dear Sandy,

I am so sorry to hear how things are with your parents. I have been praying that God would keep your dad from drinking and both of your parents from quarreling and fighting.

I don't know what I can tell you that will help

you. I don't suppose there's anything I can say that will make things any easier for you. But I do know that Jesus Christ helped me so very much at the time my dad and mom died. I know He can help you, too.

I wish I was there to explain it to you and show you some Bible verses that would help you, but I know that Pastor Reeves or his wife would be glad to talk to you about how to become a Christian. Why don't you go over and see them, Sandy? I know that Jesus can make things easier for you. He can make you and your parents Christians. He can keep your dad from drinking and help your parents to get along better than they do now.

I'll be praying for you.

DeeDee

She read the letter over again, carefully. She didn't do a very good job of explaining how Sandy could give her heart to Jesus Christ, that was sure. For a moment or two she debated whether to tear up the letter and try again, but she decided against that. She didn't have any assurance that another letter would be any better than this one. Hurriedly she stuffed the letter into an envelope and sealed it.

CHAPTER 7

A VISIT BY THE MOUNTIES

The following morning when Phil and the Davis boys went down to the dock, the boat Marcel had taken was there, tied as securely as though it had never been moved. Del went over to it and checked it thoroughly.

"When do you suppose he came back?" he asked.

His companions shook their heads.

"I don't know, but it must have been after we went to sleep," Doug said. "I didn't hear him come in." Phil was the one who noticed that the fishermen's big boat was gone.

"Those guys must have gone out fishing early this morning too," he said.

They mentioned that fact to Uncle Carl at the breakfast table, but it didn't seem to disturb him.

"A lot of fishermen around here try their luck a lot earlier than I care to go fishing," he said. "If they want to lose half a night's sleep though, it's all right with me. Just as long as they don't ask me to go along."

Del swallowed. "I've been wondering about something, Uncle Carl," he said. "You don't suppose they scooted out early because they didn't want Cap to see Marcel, do you?"

Carl stared curiously at him.

"Why would they care if Cap saw an Indian boy?" He laughed depreciatingly. "I know you'd like to make something mysterious out of it, but there's nothing out of the ordinary about an early morning fishing trip. If you ask me, there's one reason and only one reason why those guys went out so early. Someone must have told them the fish bite better just after sunup than they do any other time of the day."

Their conversation was choked off by the dramatic entrance of Mrs. Braisted. The older woman came charging across the hard ground and up the steps, her heels making an angry beat. She flung open the screen door and loomed, forbidding, in the doorway.

"Good morning, Mrs. Braisted," Carl greeted her. Her fierce gaze met his.

"Speak for yourself." Anger honed her voice to a razor edge.

Carl Orlis, who was used to meeting all sorts of people at his little fishing resort, could not keep the surprise from his face.

"Is something troubling you?" he asked.

By this time she had decided that whatever was

bothering her was not enough to keep her from the breakfast table. She stomped across the floor imperiously, her gaze flickering from one boy to the other, and jerked out her chair to sit down.

"Apparently you don't care whether I get any sleep at night or not," she snapped.

Although she directed her remark at the boys, Carl was the one who answered her.

"I don't believe I understand what you're talking about, Mrs. Braisted."

With all deliberation she straightened and pivoted to eye her host balefully.

"Do you mean to sit there and tell me that you don't *know* what I'm talking about?"

Carl's gaze met hers evenly.

"That's right," he said quietly. "I don't have the slightest idea what you're talking about."

It seemed to Del that Mrs. Braisted's face whitened by several shades. Her lips curled about the words as she spoke.

"And I don't suppose *they* know what I'm talking about either." With a jerk of her head, she indicated Doug and Del and Phil.

Eyes rounded.

"We—we sure don't know what you're so upset about, either, Mrs. Braisted," Phil said, trying to sound sincere. "Do we, guys?"

They echoed agreement with what he had said.

"Humph!" She snorted her disbelief. "I should have

known better than to have expected you to admit to anything. After all, your actions were so rude!"

Del spoke next. "But we don't know what you're talking about," he insisted. "Honestly, we don't. If we've done anything to bother you, we sure don't know what it is."

Doug nodded for emphasis.

"We're telling you the truth. We don't know why you couldn't sleep last night, but it was nothing that we did. I can tell you that much."

Carl Orlis spoke firmly. "I think you had better tell us what this is all about, Mrs. Braisted," he said. "The boys say they don't know why you were kept awake last night, and I believe them."

"Hmph!"

"If you will just tell us what happened last night," he said, "perhaps we can explain."

"There is no use in an explanation." She drew herself up haughtily. "But I can tell you this right now. If it happens again, I'm packing my things and leaving on the next boat for Warroad!"

* * *

Breakfast was always early at the Carl Orlis home the mornings that the *Island Queen* was there. The crew and whatever passengers she was taking out ate with Carl and Mary. Breakfast had to be over in time for everybody to get aboard so the little packet boat could leave at 8:00.

The kids wouldn't have had to get up that early for breakfast, but they were all there, anyway. And, as soon as Uncle Carl excused them, the boys left the table. They went out onto the dock where they sat, waiting for Cap and Kenny to come out and start the engines of the *Island Queen*. For a time, they looked in silence across the bay toward the Canadian shore.

"Mrs. Braisted was mad this morning, wasn't she?" Phil asked.

"You can say that again. I was afraid she was going to clobber all of us." Doug picked up a pebble and skipped it across the placid water. "What do you suppose she was so upset about?"

"Search me," Doug said. "But whatever it is, she's still plenty mad about it. I can tell you that much."

Phil's eyes glinted with excitement. "I think we ought to find out what's eating her, don't you?" he asked.

Cap and Kenny Stearns came out just then, and in a couple of minutes, the *Island Queen* moved cautiously away from the dock.

As though by signal, the big white fishing boat came roaring up the bay from Harrison Creek. It turned sharply to avoid the *Island Queen* and raced in the direction of the Orlis dock.

"Here come our fishermen," Phil murmured.

Del's face darkened. "I can't figure it out. They're

always gone until the *Island Queen* leaves. Then they come back."

Doug didn't think there was anything unusual about it. "It could be something that just happened. They might figure that they'd like to have breakfast, or maybe they're just tired."

Del's reply was cut short as the boat glided in to the dock.

"Hi." Marcel's grin flashed.

"Catch any fish?" Phil asked him.

"A couple."

Ralph glanced impatiently at the Indian boy.

"Snap it up. We want to get those fish filleted and the gas tank filled so we can go out again."

There was a brief hesitation. Del's gaze met Marcel's, puzzling at what he read in the young Indian's dark eyes. There were things going on that he didn't understand – things that were a little frightening to him.

Shortly before noon that day two Royal Canadian Mounted Police stopped by the Orlis home in their canoe. Carl went down to meet them and brought them up to the house.

"Now, it isn't going to do any good to argue with me," he said. "You're going to stay for dinner."

One officer's grin lifted the corners of his mouth infectiously.

"Who's arguing? I've been telling Pete ever since we were sent down here that Mary Orlis is the best cook in this part of the country. You wouldn't expect me to beat myself out of a chance to prove it, would you?"

They went in and sat down. As soon as the boys saw the canoe, they hurried inside, but not in time. The conversation they were so curious to hear was just ending.

"I've been wondering what you guys were doing down this way."

"It isn't often I get a chance to work here on the lake," one of the officers said. "The last couple of years, I've been stuck in Kenora."

"I hope you get what you're after."

"We will." He spoke confidently. "It might take a little time, but we'll close the case before we're through."

Del hitched his chair closer.

"What are you doing here?" he asked, trying to sound casual, the way Uncle Carl sounded, but he knew it didn't come off very well.

The officer laughed. "To tell you the truth, we came down here to get some of your Aunt Mary's good cooking."

Del groaned inwardly. That wasn't the answer he wanted, but it would have to do. He couldn't question the officers anymore.

Shortly after dinner the two Canadian police officers thanked Mary Orlis profusely, excused themselves, and headed back for their side of the border. Doug, Del, and Phil went out to the dock with them.

"I sure hope you get whoever you're looking for," Phil said.

The officer named Pete eyed him quizzically. "Did we say that we're looking for someone?"

Color crept into Phil's cheeks. He couldn't tell whether the officer was teasing him or not. But, before he could frame another question, the canoe was gone.

"We sure didn't find out anything from those two." Disgust edged Del's voice.

They turned to leave the dock, but Ralph White came out of the far cabin and hurried over to them.

"I see you had company."

Doug nodded.

"A couple of RCMP officers came for dinner."

"Aunt Mary thought you would be in to eat too," Del said. "Weren't you supposed to have your meals with us?"

Ralph seemed strangely disturbed and defensive. "We had breakfast on the lake this morning and, to tell you the truth, we didn't feel like eating now."

He went over and pretended to look for something in the boat.

"What were the RCMP doing here?"

Del shrugged. "As far as we know, they came over to have dinner with Aunt Mary and Uncle Carl."

Ralph's lips curled.

"You don't expect me to believe that, do you?"

"They were talking to Uncle Carl about something," Phil said, "but they wouldn't let us hear anything."

That seemed to disturb Ralph more than ever. He turned to face them. "I guess it doesn't matter. I was just curious, that's all."

With that he headed back to the cabin, leaving the boys standing there.

CHAPTER 8

EARLY MORNING BALL GAME

Edith Braisted came to the table that evening, anger bright in her eyes. Mary Orlis spoke to her.

"I'm so glad you came in to eat tonight."

Their guest mumbled something unintelligibly.

"I was concerned when you didn't come in at noon," Mary went on. "I wanted to go out and see if you were ill, but Carl thought perhaps you wanted to be alone and rest. If you hadn't come in tonight, I planned on going to your cabin to check on you."

"Humph." Her gaze met Mary's coldly. "Tell me, do *all* the stray men in the area stop here to eat?"

At first Mrs. Orlis couldn't imagine what the other woman was talking about. Her forehead wrinkled curiously. Then her eyes brightened.

"Oh, you mean Don and Pete? They only stop by when they're close. Don likes my apple pie. He says he has to stop every once in a while to get a piece of it to keep him from getting homesick. He says his mother uses the same recipe, but I think he's only teasing me."

Mrs. Braisted was not mollified.

"I would think you would have more consideration for your paying guests than to ask all of these strange men to come and eat with you. I find it positively disgusting."

Mary stared. In that part of the country, guests were always welcome. She couldn't conceive of anyone feeling otherwise.

"It so happens that I came up here because I wanted to have a certain degree of privacy," Mrs. Braisted continued acidly. "If I had known you were running a free soup kitchen, I'd have gone somewhere else."

Mary colored delicately.

"Strangers are always welcome in our home, Mrs. Braisted," she said quietly.

The other woman said no more.

Del eyed her questioningly. Like Ralph, she seemed to have an unnatural amount of interest in the appearance of the RCMP officers. He couldn't help wondering why.

The boys were more concerned than ever over the way things were developing at Angle Inlet.

"First the police came out and searched the *Island Queen* before we left Warroad. Then Ralph White and Charlie Wilson and Marcel come up here, acting as though they were afraid to have Cap and Kenny see them. Next that peculiar Mrs. Braisted comes to spend the summer and starts out by acting as though she's mad at everyone."

"Let me clue you in," Del said. "I don't think she's acting. She's *got* to be mad at everybody. She couldn't be so ornery otherwise."

"And then," Doug said, "the RCMP come over and they won't tell us what they want or why they talked so confidentially with Uncle Carl. I don't get it."

"Neither do I," his brother added. "And I don't get Mrs. Braisted's reason for not coming in and eating while they were here, either – unless she has something to hide."

Phil breathed deeply.

"It is strange," he said. "I've got to admit that. It's awfully strange."

Del moved forward until he could see Blackie just outside the front door.

"Somebody around here has got some answers – if we can just look hard enough to find them."

"Answers?" The new voice was light and mocking. "About what?"

He spun to face DeeDee and Marie. "You wouldn't understand," he retorted in disgust.

"Don't be too sure that we wouldn't understand," DeeDee said. "We probably understand a lot of things that you don't."

Excitement sparked Marie's eyes.

"You can say that again. We know a lot of things about what's going on here."

Doug spoke up. "Like what?"

"They're just feeding us a line," Phil retorted. "They don't know a thing that we don't know."

"That's what you think," Marie countered. "Do you know that the bank in Warroad was robbed?"

The boys started.

"And do you know that the authorities think the bank robbers might be coming up this way to try to sneak across the border into Canada?"

"So that's what the RCMP were doing around here today!"

"See!" Triumph gleamed in Marie's eyes. "We told you some things that you didn't know. And you're the ones who think you're so smart."

Doug was more interested in the bank robbery than in anything else.

"When did they rob the bank?" he asked. "And how much money did they get?"

"They robbed the bank three days ago," DeeDee said, "but I don't know why we're telling you these things. You won't tell us anything."

Marie broke in. "And they got more than two hundred thousand dollars in cash!"

Del looked from his brother to Phil and back again.

"That could explain a lot of things," Del said.

"If it's all true," Phil added, his doubt showing through.

"It's true, all right," Marie countered. "If you don't believe it, you can ask Uncle Carl or Kay. They were right here when the Mounties were talking about it."

"You mean you got to *hear* everything they said?" Doug demanded.

"We got to hear everything."

DeeDee turned to her cousin. "Don't tell them anything else, Marie. They think they're *so* smart! And they weren't going to tell us anything. Just let them wonder what else we found out."

Doug moved half a step closer to his sister.

"Come on, DeeDee," he pleaded. "We're sorry we treated you the way we did. Have a heart! Let us in on what you heard them say."

Her laughter was taunting.

"What makes you think I know anything more than what I've already told you?"

"Do you?"

Knowing she had him frantic with concern, she continued to tease him.

"Wouldn't you like to know?" With that she turned away. "Come on, Marie, we've wasted too much time talking to the boys already. We've got some important things to do."

The boys stared after their sisters, exasperation glinting in their eyes.

"They sure think they're smart," Del murmured.

"Just wait until we find out something. We won't let them know a thing!"

"I'm not ready to give up yet," Phil said. "I know I can't get anything more out of Marie, but I believe I can talk DeeDee into telling me what they overheard."

"Guess again. When she gets in a mood like that, she won't tell us anything. We'll have to wait for a while and then trick her into spilling what she knows."

"*If* she knows anything else," Del added.

Phil frowned indecisively. "They probably told us everything they overheard and are just trying to have some fun with us."

"Maybe," Doug replied, "and maybe not."

* * *

The following morning the boys were surprised when they went into the dining room and saw that Mrs. Braisted was there, prim and tall in a straight-backed chair, her mouth as firm and hard as thin, drawn steel.

"Good morning," Del said. He was so surprised and embarrassed that he could think of nothing else to say.

"Is it?" she demanded, eyes flashing.

Surprised, Del stared at her.

"Is–is there something wrong?"

Arrogantly, she drew herself up.

"You ought to know, young man!"

Still staring, he went over and sat down across from her. For the space of a minute or two, no one spoke.

The boys glanced at each other uneasily. At last Mrs. Braisted turned to Del once more. She spoke icily.

"I hope you enjoyed your ball game this morning." Acid dripped from her tongue.

The Davis boy gasped.

"What ball game?"

"You don't have to act so innocent with me. You were out playing baseball this morning right behind my cabin!"

"We were in bed until just a little while ago, Mrs. Braisted. We couldn't have been out behind your cabin playing baseball."

"That's right." Phil added his word to Del's. "Besides, Mr. Orlis wouldn't let us play baseball behind the cabins early in the morning and waken the guests, even if we wanted to."

Her gaze fastened owlishly on him.

"I don't know what you hope to gain by lying, young man, but I am not altogether stupid. I know what was going on behind my cabin this morning. And I know that I was awakened and lay for almost two hours before it was time to get up!"

The boys shook their heads in silence.

CHAPTER 9

A STRANGE CONVERSATION

Uncle Carl had chores for the Davis boys and Phil to do all morning at the Angle, so it wasn't until after lunch that the three boys could talk together without being overheard. They were more perplexed than ever about Mrs. Braisted.

"Let me tell you," Doug said, his indignation rising, "there's something wrong with that woman in the brains department. Imagine, thinking someone was playing baseball outside her cabin at 4:00 in the morning! She must be off her rocker!"

Phil picked up a twig and broke it in two.

"That's not the only thing that's strange about her," he said.

"What do you mean?"

"Have you noticed that she doesn't want to make friends with anyone? She hardly speaks to Ralph or Charlie when she meets them, and she doesn't treat the rest of us much better. I've never seen anyone so unsociable. She acts as though we've got leprosy or something."

Del had scarcely been listening to them.

"If something isn't done to make her happier," he observed, "she's not likely to be around the place long enough to speak to any of us."

Doug shrugged indifferently.

"I can't say that I'd lose any sleep if she did leave here on the *Island Queen* day after tomorrow. I'd say it was good riddance."

"Maybe it would be, but Uncle Carl needs the money she'll be paying for board and the rental of the cabin this summer. And if somebody doesn't do something, she's apt to leave. Right now, she acts as though she's mad enough to go storming out of here and never come back."

Doug frowned momentarily. What Del said about Uncle Carl and Aunt Mary needing the money Edith Braisted was paying them was true. He had overheard them talking about it a day or so before. The money would pay their taxes, Uncle Carl had said.

"We've got to do something to get Mrs. Braisted straightened out so she'll stay."

Phil stood up.

"That sounds good, but what are we going to do? That's what I'd like to know."

The corners of Del's mouth tightened. "We've got to find out what she was talking about when she was complaining about a baseball game going on early this morning."

Doug nodded. "Y'know, I just thought of something. Marcel just might be able to help us."

Phil spoke up quickly. "You don't think he's been waking up Mrs. Braisted, do you?"

"Him?" Doug snorted indignantly. "Who would Marcel be playing baseball with at 4:00 in the morning? Even if he wanted to." Doug breathed deeply. "I just figured that if there was something out by her cabin this morning, Marcel and his friends may have heard it, that's all. They're sleeping in the cabin next to hers."

"I think you've got a point there," Del told him.

Phil moved restlessly. When he had something on his mind, he wanted to take care of it.

"Well, if we're going to find him, let's get moving," he said. "We aren't going to accomplish anything by standing here."

The boys checked the dock first to see if Marcel was out fishing with the men he was guiding, but the big white boat was there, secured to the pier.

"Well, he's not out fishing. We know that much."

"Maybe he's gone off to one of the islands in one of Uncle Carl's boats to visit some of his friends. He did that once, you know."

Del shook his head.

"I don't think so. Uncle Carl told him not to take one of the boats again unless he got permission first.

I think he understood that he'd better not try that again."

Phil spoke up quickly. "Besides, all the boats are in." He glanced around. "There's no other way for him to leave. He's got to be around some place."

"Maybe Mrs. Braisted scared him away," Del observed. "She's got me to the place where I feel like I'd as soon crawl down a hole as have to stay and talk to her."

"You and me both."

The boys went behind the house to the path that led to the narrow pasture that marked the edge of the clearing and to the school two miles away.

"There's still no sign of him."

Del spoke up. "I don't think this is going to help us a bit. He won't know anything, and he probably won't tell us if he does."

"I–" Phil stopped quickly. "There's someone over there!" His voice was a harsh whisper.

Instinctively the boys crouched, their breath stopped in their throats and their shoulders jerking convulsively. It was a moment or two before anyone spoke.

"Are–are you sure?" Doug's voice was so soft they were scarcely able to make out what he said, yet they were afraid that whoever was in the brush had heard them as well. "Are you sure?"

Phil nodded.

"I'm positive!" He pointed with a wavering forefinger.

Del stared in the direction he was pointing, but he could hear nothing. All was silent now – a strange, taut silence that somehow seemed to increase in intensity with each agonizing minute.

"I–I don't see anything!" Del whispered.

Phil's dark eyes narrowed. "Neither do I, but there's someone over there just the same."

He inched forward cautiously into the brush with Doug and Del half a step behind. They moved quietly, easing their feet into the soft ferns. Every now and then they stopped to listen. At first, they could hear nothing except the wind moving restlessly in the treetops.

Del looked about, relaxing slightly as he saw that there was nothing out of the ordinary within seeing distance at least. Perhaps Phil had heard something he thought were voices. It could have been an animal or maybe the wind. He was about to speak aloud, voicing his doubts, when the sound came again. This time there was no mistaking it. They jerked to a halt!

"You don't know how much I've missed you," they heard a woman say.

"I've missed you too."

Del felt the sweat come out on his forehead. His breathing was quick and shallow. The woman's voice! He would recognize it anywhere!

For half a minute or more the Davis boys and Phil

remained motionless, their entire beings frozen. The man and woman who were talking nearby continued in guarded tones.

"It's been so hard seeing you and having to act as though I don't even know you," the woman went on.

The man retorted quickly. "Shh! Somebody might hear you!"

"Who would hear us way out here? We're a quarter of a mile from the house!"

There was a brief hesitation.

"Who is it?" Doug whispered in his brother's ear.

"Don't you know?" Del's lips formed the words. "It's Mrs. Braisted and Charlie Wilson!"

Before Del could finish answering his cousin, Phil jabbed him in the ribs in warning. The couple was talking again.

"Are you sure you weren't seen coming out here?" Charlie asked.

"Don't get so upset. Nobody saw me. I made sure of that before I came."

Charlie was irritable. "I hope you're right! If you were followed out here, it could ruin everything."

The boys involuntarily crouched lower, as though Charlie had suddenly become aware of their presence and had started searching for them.

"How much longer will it be?" she asked.

"I don't know yet. But you'd better get back to camp before someone misses you."

They started directly toward the Davis boys and

Phil. The boys silently dove frantically into the brush and lay motionless on their stomachs. And just in time. A split second after they scrambled for cover, Charlie and Mrs. Braisted walked by on their way back to the Orlis cabins.

"You'd better go on ahead, Edith," he told her. "I'll stay in the trees until I get to the creek so I can come back to the cabins from a different direction."

Phil rose on one elbow in time to see that they were holding hands when they disappeared from view.

"I thought we were going to get caught before we could find a place to hide," Doug said, still trembling.

Del stood and then spoke thoughtfully. "You know," he observed curiously, "I'd give a lot to know what that was all about."

"Me too," Phil said. "There's got to be some good reason why those two don't want anyone to know that they're acquainted with each other."

Doug leaned forward, his voice coming out in a hoarse whisper. "I've been wondering about that bank robbery in Warroad. You don't suppose this could have anything to do with it, do you?"

The other two jerked up, their cheeks blanching.

"I never thought of that!" Del exclaimed.

"Neither did I!"

Del moved forward uncertainly, as though he didn't know what to do. It didn't make sense that Charlie Wilson and Edith Braisted were bank robbers.

"They don't look as though they would steal anything."

Doug's impatience showed through.

"Maybe they don't and maybe they do." He paused momentarily. "How many bank robbers have you ever seen?"

Del acted as though he hadn't even heard his brother.

"But why would they come up to stay at a place like this? That's what I can't figure out. You'd think they would want to get as far away as they could. At least, if I'd just robbed a bank, that's what I'd want to do."

"That's the way I figured at first," Doug told him. "But then I got to thinking that maybe they would be safer close by than they would be trying to run. The authorities wouldn't expect them to be right here at Warroad's back door. They might figure a place like this is just where to stay until the police quit looking so hard for them."

Phil nodded.

"I think you've got something there." He waited so long before he spoke again that neither Del nor Doug expected him to say anything else. "At least there's something mighty strange going on between those two," he said.

"You can say that again."

Phil's determination firmed his jaw. "And we've got to find out what it's all about! That's all there is to it!"

CHAPTER 10

ONE MYSTERY SOLVED

The three boys made their way back to the Orlis home as cautiously as Charlie Wilson and Edith Braisted did. They, too, wanted to be sure that no one saw them emerging from the forest, and especially that Mrs. Braisted and Charlie didn't see them. They darted out of the wood and sauntered up to the house with affected carelessness, as though they had been out back to look at the rabbits. As they neared the back door, DeeDee and Marie came out to meet them.

"Oh, there you are," DeeDee said.

"Hi." Del tried to sound casual, but he knew that guilt tinged his voice and he hoped they didn't notice it.

"Where have you been?" his sister demanded. "We've been looking all over for you."

Doug answered, "Just around."

"You weren't anywhere in the yard," Marie said, her manner accusing. "We looked and looked for you."

Phil spoke, using the tone brothers so often reserve for their younger sisters. "Can't we even go out for a little walk without having to face an inquisition when we get back? We haven't broken any laws, Marie. You don't have to give us the third degree."

"What we really wanted was to tell you that Uncle Carl has been wanting to talk to you."

Del's eyes widened.

"Why didn't you say so?"

"You were too busy finding fault with everything we were saying to listen to us."

They went into the house where Carl was sitting in front of the fireplace. The boys spoke to him. He looked up, managing a smile.

"Did you want to talk to us?" Del asked.

"I wanted to tell you that Mrs. Braisted will be leaving in the morning."

The boys stared.

"What?"

"She said that she can't stand the noise around here so early in the morning."

"Noise?" Doug's voice rose. "What noise?"

"Is she still complaining about someone playing baseball at 4:00 in the morning?"

"Among other things," Uncle Carl said. "Now she claims she hears a dog barking and somebody yelling along the creek bank."

Del exploded. "I don't think she hears anything at all. I think she just wants to find fault."

"Perhaps, but we can't argue with her. I just wanted to ask you boys to get up a little earlier than usual in the morning and help get her luggage on the *Island Queen.*"

"Sure. Sure thing."

Once outside, the boys huddled excitedly.

"What do you make of this?" Del asked.

Doug shook his head. "I don't know. It makes me wonder if she isn't using that as an excuse to leave!"

In their room that evening Del, Doug, and Phil stayed awake for a long while talking about the strange things that had happened at the Orlis place since they arrived. They had been thinking of little else since they overheard Mrs. Braisted and Charlie Wilson talking to each other out in the woods, but they were still as far from a solution as ever. There didn't seem to be any answer to the question that kept crowding into their minds.

"I can't figure it out," Phil said. "One minute Mrs. Braisted is out in the woods talking to a fisherman she claimed never to have seen before. They sound like long-lost buddies who've got a big deal on. And the next thing we know, she's planning on leaving in the morning. I don't get it." In the semidarkness of the bedroom, he looked at his companions curiously. "I've gone over it a hundred times, but it doesn't make sense to me."

Doug shrugged. "You're not alone. It doesn't make sense to me either."

Del rolled over on his back and sat up. He did not speak immediately, but when he did his voice was serious.

"Did it ever occur to you that there might not be any mystery about Mrs. Braisted at all?" he asked. "Maybe she's just exactly what she says she is."

"What do you mean?" his brother wanted to know.

"Maybe she did come up here to spend the three weeks the way she said she did the afternoon she came in on the *Island Queen*."

Phil spoke up thoughtfully. "I suppose that could be the deal," he said, "but I sure don't think so. It doesn't square with what we heard her say in the woods this afternoon when she was talking to Charlie. It sounded, then, like they have some big deal going that depends on nobody finding out that they know each other."

"That's just the point," Del said. "Nothing in this whole affair squares with anything else. It's all one big, jumbled mess that doesn't add up."

"That's the thing that grabs me," Phil retorted. "Nothing adds up. And it ought to. There must be some reasons for these things."

Doug swung his feet over the side of the bed.

"I'm with you, Phil. There's something strange going on here, and we've got to find out what it is."

Del scratched his ear. He had to admit that he agreed with Doug too. And he was sure that things would add up if they could only unravel the tangled mess. Only, how could they find out anything more when Edith Braisted was going back to Warroad on the *Island Queen* the next morning?

"There's a fat chance of finding out what's going on now," Del said. "She's pulling out. Remember?"

"Maybe we can stop her."

Del laughed mirthlessly. "And just exactly how are you going to be able to accomplish that? The way I see it, we'd have just about as much chance of stopping a ten-ton truck as we'd have stopping her if she's got her mind made up about something."

Doug thought for a time. "We can start by getting up at 4:00 in the morning and try to find out what it is that she's kicking up such a fuss about."

Doug set the alarm for a little before 4:00 and put the alarm on the floor just out of reach.

"I don't know what we're going to find out at that hour, but I guess it won't hurt to try."

Phil crawled into bed.

"You know, there's something we're forgetting in all of this. If Mrs. Braisted is using the early morning noises as an excuse for getting out of here, we're not going to find out anything by getting up early in the morning. And we're not going to get her to stay here by proving that there isn't any 4 a.m. ball game."

Del thought about that momentarily.

"I think you've got a point," he admitted, "but it's the only chance we've got."

* * *

The next morning Doug groped for the jangling alarm clock.

Phil rose up on one elbow. "Shut that thing off, Doug. You'll wake up the whole household!"

Doug stumbled out of bed and felt for the clock until he found it and silenced its strident ringing.

Del swung his feet over the side of his bed. "That's the loudest alarm clock I've ever heard."

"Any alarm clock is loud at 4:00 in the morning."

Doug switched on his flashlight.

"Pipe down, you guys!" he warned. "You'll have Uncle Carl and Aunt Mary and Kay on our necks if you aren't careful."

Del was still grumbling as he began to dress.

"It won't be us. It'll be that stupid alarm clock of yours."

The trio dressed in silence and made their way as quietly as possible out into the still air. Del shivered in the early morning breeze.

"I wish I'd brought my jacket. It's cold out here."

"We can't go back for it now," Phil told him. "If we did, we'd waken everybody for sure." As he spoke, he started in the direction of Mrs. Braisted's cabin.

Dawn would not be long in coming. The first faint gray messengers from the sun were etching themselves outward from the eastern horizon, streaking the cloudless sky. The darkness was even now beginning to disappear. First, its black intensity softened. Then the boys could make out the outline of the trees beyond the tourist cabins. While they crouched there expectantly, the opposite shore of the creek began to appear out of the shadows.

"Well, it's about time for Mrs. Braisted's baseball game to start if it's going to," Doug said in a hoarse whisper.

"Don't hold your breath until it does," Phil cautioned.

"Shh!" Del put a finger to his lips in warning. "It'll be just our luck to have her catch us out here this morning. And if she does, we'll never be able to make her believe we haven't been out here every morning playing ball just to torment her."

At that instant, as though on signal, it began.

"Play ball!" The voice was shrill and arrogant.

Del gasped.

"Play ball! Strike one! Ball one! Play ball! Play ball!"

Phil grasped Doug by the arm. "Do you hear what I hear?"

"Run, Doug! Run! Run!"

"Blackie!" Del stood up, his hands on his hips. "It's that stupid crow of mine! He's the one who has caused all the trouble."

Phil laughed. "I guess Mrs. Braisted did hear something after all."

"Blackie!" He called guardedly to his pet crow.

"Blackie! Shut up and come here or I'll wring your stupid neck!"

Blackie seemed to sense that he had an audience, and his arrogance grew.

"You're out, Doug! Play ball! Play ball!"

Doug and Phil snickered.

"You sure did a good job of training him," Phil whispered. "That's all I can say!"

At that moment a dark figure appeared at the window.

"This time I've caught you!" Edith Braisted exclaimed triumphantly.

Before the boys could reply, there was a muffled sound at the dock. Phil spun about.

"Did you hear that?" he demanded.

"Did we hear what?"

"Somebody's taking one of Uncle Carl's boats!"

CHAPTER 11

KIDNAPPED!

Phil, Doug, and Del froze where they were standing, listening with an intentness they were not even aware of. The sound came again, the muffled thumping of wood against wood. There was something indefinably stealthy about it as though the individual who was making the noise was trying desperately not to.

It was only a few seconds until Phil spoke once more, but it seemed an hour, so acutely alert were the three boys.

"Did–did you hear that?" Phil's voice came out in a thin, unnatural squeak. "I tell you, guys, there's somebody down at the boats!"

For a tense, electric instant the boys waited breathlessly, staring at each other.

"Maybe it's Marcel or his fishermen getting ready to go out on the lake again this morning. They go out early, you know," Doug said, his tone revealing that he didn't really believe that it was Marcel and his companions.

"It couldn't be them," Del said. "They left last night. Remember?"

"That's right." Charlie and Ralph and Marcel had left after supper the evening before to go back to Warroad for something, so it couldn't be them.

"Or," Del went on almost hopefully, "or, maybe it's Cap or someone else on the *Island Queen* who couldn't sleep this morning."

Phil shook his head. "Who would be up at this hour fooling around with a boat?" he asked.

Doug grinned in spite of himself.

"Maybe Blackie taught one of his brothers or his cousins to talk too, so he won't have to talk to Del all the time."

Del snorted. "Very funny!"

Phil started forward cautiously with Del and Doug close behind.

"Whoever's down there hasn't got any business fooling with those boats."

"Maybe we ought to go and call Uncle Carl," Doug said.

"If we take time for that, the guy'll have one of the boats and be gone! We've got to stop him ourselves or he'll get away!"

Mrs. Braisted called something to them as they disappeared from view, but they didn't hear what she was saying. They crept stealthily around the corner of the oil shed, eyes searching the creek bank on either side of the dock. The *Island Queen* was berthed where she usually was, blocking half of the opposite side from view.

"Take it easy!" A hoarse whisper drifted to the boys on the still morning air. "Do you want to wake everyone up?"

"Shut up and help me, will you? We've got to get out of here, pronto!"

"You should have thought about that when you stove in the bottom of our boat on a rock back there a couple of miles."

"That's all I've heard since it happened. You're alive and you ain't in jail yet, are you?"

"No thanks to you. First you try to drown me and then you try to walk me to death through that muskeg!"

"Shut up and help me!"

Phil ran forward. "You there!"

At that instant a snarling voice rasped behind them. "Pipe down and don't move!"

Phil felt something hard and round pressing into the small of his back. The strength fled from his legs, leaving him all but helpless.

Half a second later a tall, gangling stranger came into view around the stern of the *Island Queen*. A deep scowl disfigured his face.

"What's going on, Elmer?" he asked.

"I caught these kids spying on you."

Neither Phil nor the Davis boys had seen any of the men before.

"We weren't spying on anybody. We heard a noise down here and came down to see what was going on. That's all."

"And that's where you made your mistake," Elmer snarled. "You should've stayed in bed where you belong."

With that the other man found his voice.

"That's right! And now get out on the dock and be quick about it! We haven't got all day!"

Del glanced quickly over his shoulder. "W-why do you want us to g-g-go out on the dock, anyway?" he asked.

Doug broke in. "Y-you aren't going to take us along with you, are you?"

A third man who was in the boat hissed a warning.

"Pipe down, you guys! You'll have everybody in the place awake!"

"What–"

Phil started to speak loudly, but the man called Milt jabbed the gun harder in his back.

"Pipe down, you guys! We'll do the talking!"

Bart straightened slowly. "What are we goin' to do with them?"

"What can we do?" Milt asked. "We've got to take 'em along!"

The three strangers pushed the Davis boys and

Phil into the big, flat-bottomed boat and shoved away from the dock.

"You know you can't get away with this," Del said between clenched teeth.

"What makes you think that we can't?" He jerked the starter rope, and the big engine leaped to life with a roar. The boat sped across the mirrored surface of the creek in the direction of the bay. "We're getting away with it, ain't we?"

Doug broke in. "Maybe you're getting away with it right now, but that's not going to mean a thing. You won't for very long. Uncle Carl and Cap and everybody on the place is probably awake right now. They'll get the cops after you so quick you won't know what hit you."

Milt laughed, but without emotion.

"Maybe," he said, "but they've got to find us first."

"They'll find you. Don't worry about that," Phil told him.

Milt brought the cumbersome boat half around in a wide, sweeping arc and headed in the direction of the big lake and the Canadian waters.

"They ain't done so well the last ten days or so, buddy-boy. We've been right here on the Angle since we knocked off that bank, and they ain't found us yet."

Bart snarled in warning. "What's the matter with you, Milt? Can't you keep that fat lip of yours buttoned? Do you have to spill everything you know?"

The man at the outboard motor swore angrily.

"You take care of yourself and quit getting so worked up about what I'm doing. Okay?"

Doug continued. "It'd be bad enough to have a bank-robbing charge against you. Now they'll get you for kidnapping too. I sure wouldn't want to be in your shoes!"

Bart swore at him.

"Shut your mouth, kid, or I'll shut it for you!"

Two hours passed while the cumbersome flat-bottomed boat plowed through the still water. The sun was glinting over the treetops when they heard the low, vibrant hum of a light plane in the distance.

Elmer put up his hand suddenly.

"What's that?" he demanded.

"What's what?" As Milt spoke, he cut back the throttle. For half a minute the three men strained to hear the aircraft engine.

Phil spoke triumphantly. "What'd we tell you? They're coming to look for us already!"

"I told you to shut your mouth!" Milt lashed out swiftly with his open hand, catching Phil on the side of the head. He hit him so hard he almost knocked him off the boat seat.

"What'd you do that for?" the boy demanded, his eyes blazing.

"I told you to shut up or you'd be sorry!"

Bart broke in. "We'd better all shut up and do some fast scrambling or they're going to have us right here in the open lake."

Milt opened the throttle and headed for the nearest island. An instant later the plane came into view.

Del looked up. It was the RCMP Cessna 180. A silent prayer went up from his heart.

Dear God! he prayed inwardly. *Help them to see us!*

While the three boys watched prayerfully, an RCMP float plane appeared over the far horizon. The plane was only a speck when they were first able to make it out – a fly silhouetted against a distant ceiling. Del closed his eyes momentarily, his lips moving, but without sound.

The men were watching too, eyes following the aircraft as it drew nearer. Desperation flushed their cheeks and set their lips to quivering. They were still a quarter of a mile from the nearest island. Bart apparently considered himself the trio's leader. He glanced quickly at Milt who was operating the outboard motor; his voice was harsh with fear when he spoke.

"Hurry it up, will you? We're sitting ducks out here! They're going to spot us at any second!"

Milt swore nervously but reached back and pushed on the throttle.

"And just what do you think I'm doing? Answer me that! I've got this lousy motor wide open now!"

Del cast a quick glance back at Elmer, who seemed to be transfixed with fright.

"You'd just as well give up right now. You're not going to get away. They'll catch you sooner or later."

Bart exploded. "One more crack like that and you'll

wish you hadn't opened your stupid little mouth!"
He raised his fist in warning.

The boat was only a hundred yards from the
island, but the airplane was gaining rapidly. By this
time, the boys could make out the insignia on the
plane. It was all Phil could do to keep from waving
frantically.

"It's the RCMP, all right!"

"I told you to shut up!"

Bart swung at Phil, but he ducked away, rocking
the boat dangerously. Milt yelled in protest.

"Bart, are you out of your mind?" He swore again,
savagely. "You'll spill us all in the water and ruin
everything!"

At that instant Milt shut off the motor. The large
boat glided to a stop under a heavy growth of brush
that hung low over the water. The brush was so thick
and so close to the surface of the lake that the occu-
pants in the boat practically had to lie down.

For some time, they all remained motionless,
breathing heavily. It seemed an hour before anyone
spoke. Then Elmer sighed his immense relief.

"We made it!" he exclaimed.

Bart sneered at him. "I told you that we'd make
it, didn't I?"

"You told us a lot of things!"

"Maybe you'd like to get out of the deal right now.
How about it?"

"You know better'n that!"

"Then shut up and do as I say. I told you that we're going to make it! Everything's going to work out fine. You just do what old Bart says and you'll see!"

Milt spoke – still irritably. "Yeah, you told us that we'd make it, all right. But you've told us a lot of things that haven't worked out the way you said they would. You told us we could steal a boat and motor from old man Orlis without anyone finding out about it, too. Or have you forgotten that already?"

A defensive note crept into the self-styled leader's voice.

"How was I to know that these stupid kids were going to be running around so early in the morning?"

Milt held up a hand for silence.

"It's not going to do us any good to keep fighting this way. Besides, I want to listen to that plane! I want to find out if it's going on or if they saw us and are circling."

The little group listened intently.

Feeling his leg cramp, Del moved in an effort to get into a more comfortable position. In doing so he bumped against the side of the boat. A hard object in his pocket startled him so much that he almost cried out.

His pocketknife! And along the floor beneath the boat seats ran the rubber fuel line from the remote tank to the outboard motor. He paused, raising his head slightly and looking around. The brush was making them all so uncomfortable that no one was paying much attention to anyone else. If he could only get his hand in his pocket without being seen and get that knife out!

Stealthily he moved. As he did so he kicked Bart's arm.

"You, there!" the man snarled. "Cut that out!"

Breathlessly, Del stopped.

"What're you trying to do, anyway?"

No answer.

"I'm warnin' you guys! You'd better quit makin' me mad if you know what's good for you!"

"I–I didn't mean to kick you!"

Del waited until the men began to talk among themselves. Then, with great stealth, he shifted his weight so he could get his fingers on the cold, hard knife. Now, all he had to do was to get it out of his pocket and get it open.

The Davis boy worked fearfully, but the three men were too concerned about their own problems to pay much attention to their unwilling guests.

"How long do you figure we're going to have to hide out?"

"That's just what I was wondering," Elmer asked.

Bart, whose authority had been threatened only moments before, resumed command once more.

"We'll have to stick around here until after sundown. They won't fly that plane after dark."

Elmer wasn't sure that he liked the idea.

"We've got a long way to go to get back to the

place where we left that box. I don't much like wastin' all this time."

Bart's voice rose in a sneer. "I suppose you'd rather get caught and get sent back to the pen." Bart's anger seemed to soften. "You don't have to get so upset, Elmer. As soon as it's safe, we're going back after the box, then we'll slip up here, make our way to Kenora and be long gone."

"We should've kept the box with us like I wanted to," Milt protested. "Then we wouldn't have to worry about going back after it."

The leader of the ugly-tempered trio started to speak but seemed to change his mind. When he did, his words were almost mild.

"As it worked out, it would have been better if we'd brought the box along; but we didn't, so now we've got to do the next best thing. We've got to go back after it!"

Holding the knife cautiously, Del groped for the gas line. At first, he planned to cut it in two; but as he was about to do so, he decided against it. Cutting the gas line would scarcely delay them at all, he reasoned. They would be able to find a severed gasoline line in a moment or two and repair it in about the same length of time it would take him to cut it. A lot of little holes would be much better. They would be harder to spot.

CHAPTER 12

TIME TO PRAY!

Back at Angle Inlet, Carl had heard the outboard motor start that morning and roar away. He turned sleepily on his side.

"Mary?"

She stirred.

"Mary," he repeated, "did you hear that?"

"Hear what?" She was only half awake.

"An outboard motor started."

She rolled over and closed her eyes once more. "It's just somebody going fishing. Lie down and go back to sleep. It's much too early to get up."

Carl lay down, but only for an instant or two. Then he rose on one elbow.

"I'd still like to know who's going fishing at this hour."

"You know how crazy these people are who like

to fish. Some of them go out at all hours of the day or night."

That seemed to help him make up his mind. He got up and reached for his pants.

"Maybe so," he retorted, "but I'm going down and take a look just the same. I've got an awfully uneasy feeling about it."

A moment later he went out the front door, still buttoning his shirt.

Carl didn't know why he was so uneasy. He felt almost embarrassed now at his concern because what Mary had said about fishermen was true. They were always getting up at the craziest hours. He ought to know that; he'd spent most of his life renting cabins to fishermen. He was half the distance to the dock when he became aware that somebody was down there, staring along the creek at the mirrored bay.

"Mrs. Braisted!" he exclaimed.

She whirled. "Mr. Orlis! You startled me!"

Carl laughed. "I guess I could say the same thing about you. I didn't expect to find you out of bed at this hour."

Edith Braisted fingered the buttons on her robe uneasily. "I'm so glad you're up. I was about to come and waken you and Mrs. Orlis."

His eyes widened.

"Did you hear the boat leave too?"

"Hear it?" Her voice trembled. "I saw them put the boys in the boat and go racing away!"

"The boys?" Carl exclaimed, fear gripping him icily. "What happened?"

Hurriedly she related what had taken place. She was still talking when Carl started for the house.

"Where are you going?" she asked.

"I'm going to get on the radio and get the authorities up here! Those boys are in terrible danger!"

* * *

After four hours of lying cramped in the boat, Milt groaned aloud.

"I tell you, Bart, my back's goin' to break in two if we don't get out of this boat. What're you trying to do? Kill us all off?"

"I don't like it any better'n you do," Bart retorted testily. "But I just don't happen to want to get caught, so we're stayin' right here."

Milt thought about that for a moment.

"It's been four hours since that plane's been around. They didn't see anything, or they'd have nailed us a long time ago."

Bart parted the brush with his hands and got painfully to his feet.

"I guess it wouldn't hurt for us to go up on the island, at least for a while."

They all got out of the boat, stretching their cramped leg muscles. Doug glanced quickly at his companions as he crawled over the side of the flat-bottomed boat. Del and Phil both saw that he was considering trying to escape, but the tingling pain in his legs when he stood up made him give up the idea. He knew they would have grabbed him before he got a dozen steps away.

Bart led the group up the steep, rocky island.

"How much longer before we go for that box?" Milt wanted to know.

Bart glanced at the sun that was riding high above them.

"I'll wait until dark before I go."

The other two stared suspiciously at him.

"Who said you were going to get to go back for it?" Elmer demanded. "I'll go!"

Milt spoke up. "I'll go!"

Doug laughed. "What's the matter with you guys? Don't you trust one another?"

They glared at him but fell silent.

The three men forced the boys to go with them up the steep, tree-covered slope. Bart, who had gone on ahead, waited for them at a small spot that was almost devoid of trees.

"How does this look to you as a place to keep the kids until I get back?"

Milt corrected him. "Until *we* get back. Elmer and I are going along, remember?"

Bart's evil face darkened. "What's the matter with you? Don't you two trust me?"

Milt laughed mirthlessly. "I trust you just about

as far as you trust me." His smile fled. "I don't trust nobody. I thought you knew that by this time."

The men argued bitterly about who was to go back for the package. Neither Milt nor Elmer would agree to letting Bart go alone. And he didn't want either of them to go unless he was along.

"We can't all go. Somebody's got to stay here and look after these stupid kids."

Elmer sneered. "Bringing them along was your idea, remember? If you want them taken care of, you can take care of them yourself."

"You can bet it was my idea to bring 'em along," Bart countered. "If I hadn't, we'd all be in handcuffs by this time and headed for prison instead of arguing about who's going back to pick up our money."

Milt's anger flared. "You'd just as well stow that kind of talk. It's not going to get you anywhere. We're not going to agree to let you go back for our dough alone!"

"All right!" Bart swore. "All right! We'll tie the kids up and all three of us will go back after it! Does that satisfy you?"

"Tie us up?" Del's concern edged his voice. "If you tie us up and leave us, how're we going to get loose after you're gone?"

"That's your problem!"

Doug spoke up. "If you leave us tied, we might starve."

"Shut up and put your hands behind your back!"

He pulled the rope so tightly around Doug's wrist that it bit into the flesh.

* * *

As soon as Carl finished sending the radio message, he started for the dock. Cap called after him.

"Where're you going, Carl?"

"I'm going out to look for those boys!"

"I'll go with you!"

The two men hurried down to the water's edge together. Carl was going to get into one of his boats, but Cap insisted that they take the *Island Queen*.

"I can go almost as fast as one of your boats," he said, "and I've got a lot more range. We can stay out all day with the *Island Queen* if we have to."

"What about your schedule? You're supposed to go down to Warroad today."

Cap loosed the stern line.

"You don't need to think I'm going to go back to Warroad until we find out what's happened to those boys."

The two gray-haired men started the packet boat's engine and cast off. The *Island Queen* came around and sped out of the mouth of Pine Creek with surprising speed.

Kay and DeeDee and Marie watched them go, tears trembling on their eyelids. Mrs. Braisted saw them and went over to where they were standing.

"Is there anything I can do?" There was genuine concern in her voice.

Kay shook her head.

"No, thank you. There's nothing anyone can do right now."

It only seemed natural that Edith Braisted would go into the house with them. Mrs. Orlis was inside, her eyes fixed on the girls. Marie flew to her, a sob choking in her throat.

"Oh, Aunt Mary!" Her arms clung to the older woman's waist.

Mary knelt beside her and put an arm around her shoulder comfortingly.

"There now, don't be so concerned. Everything's going to be all right."

"But they've got Phil and Del and Doug! And nobody knows what they'll do to them!"

By this time Marie was crying openly. For a while Mary allowed her to cry, holding her close. Finally, she spoke.

"You know, Marie, this is something we should be talking to God about."

The girl looked up curiously. She acted as though she wanted to speak but didn't know quite what to say. Mrs. Braisted, who had been watching in silence, could contain herself no longer.

"Just exactly what do you mean, Mrs. Orlis?" she asked.

The gray-haired woman's smile seemed to light up her entire being.

"We make a habit of praying about our problems."

"Oh," Edith retorted. She did not pursue the matter further.

Kay read a passage from the Bible, and they all knelt – all, that is, except Edith Braisted. She remained standing, shifting her weight nervously from one foot to the other.

CHAPTER 13

ESCAPE AND EXPLANATIONS

On the island across the Canadian line in the Lake of the Woods, Del and Doug and Phil were alone. The three men had left moments before after tying the boys securely with their hands behind their backs. Phil was the first to speak.

"Now what are we going to do?"

"For a starter, you can scoot my direction and try to get one of your hands in my pocket."

Phil stared at him.

"What?"

"I've got a knife, if we can just get at it."

Doug and Phil spoke almost at the same time. "Here! Let me try!"

"I'm closer," Phil said. "I'll get it!"

They heard the outboard motor start.

"I thought you said you had fixed that motor of theirs so it wouldn't run," Doug exclaimed.

"I did." A grin pulled at one corner of his mouth.

"What's it doing now? Answer me that."

"Just wait a jiffy and you'll find out!"

Getting the knife out of Del's pocket was more of a job than Phil had thought it would be. He had to work by feel, for one thing. And for another, his other hand kept getting in the way. But, at last his fingers closed about the heavy knife handle.

"I've got it!" he cried. "I've got it!"

"Great! Now, see if you can open the blade and cut the ropes that my hands are tied with."

While they were working, the outboard motor quit suddenly.

"There!" Del cried triumphantly. "What'd I tell you?"

At that instant Phil succeeded in freeing Del. A moment later the three of them were loose.

"Now what do we do, Del?" Phil asked.

His cousin scrambled for the brush.

"We'd better get a move on before those big play-mates of ours come back up here!"

"That," Doug said, "is the best idea you've had all day."

As they made their way hurriedly down the steep slope, Phil questioned Del about the outboard motor he had disabled.

"I didn't even see you touch it. How did you man-age to knock it out, anyway?"

"It wasn't so hard. I just jabbed about fifty holes in the rubber gas line, that's all."

"They ought to be able to fix that, hadn't they?" Doug put in.

"If they can find out what's wrong with it, they can, but it might take them a while."

Phil grinned. "I'm sure glad that I've got one smart cousin."

He was joking when he spoke, but the smile faded from Doug's face. Just because Del happened to come up with an idea or two that helped them out of the jam they were in, it was no sign he was so all-fired smart. It didn't take an honor student to have a jackknife in his pocket. In spite of himself, Doug's jealousy rose.

For a minute or two the boys did not speak. Phil turned to face his cousins.

"Now, what are we going to do?" he asked.

"I don't know," Doug retorted, "but we can't stay here, that's for sure."

Phil frowned. "Where's that island where the Indians live? The one Uncle Carl was telling about?"

Del shrugged. "It's around here somewhere."

"What good would it do us if we did know where it was?" Doug put in. "We don't have any way of getting over there."

Phil picked up a rock and skittered it along the rocky ground.

"You know," he murmured, "somebody's bound to be out looking for us by this time."

"But how're they going to find us? That's what I'd like to know. There's about a million islands in the Lake of the Woods."

"We could start a fire with plenty of black smoke," Phil continued. "That ought to bring them in a hurry."

"It'd probably bring Bart and his buddies too," Doug protested.

"They already *know* where we are," Phil answered.

"You've got a point there," Del said. "What have we got to lose?"

Hurriedly they broke branches off the dead trees nearby and started a fire. Once it was blazing high, they threw green twigs and grass on it. Acrid black smoke spiraled upward.

"Look at that!" Del exclaimed gleefully. "They'll be able to see that fire halfway to Minneapolis."

* * *

In a fire tower a dozen miles or so away, the tower man saw the first plume of smoke. He noted the direction and picked up the phone on his two-way radio.

"Looks like we've got us some trouble, Joe. There's a fire on Smith Island. Over."

"A bad one?"

"Could be. Looks like that end of the province is

on fire. You'd better get a plane over there right away and have a look at it."

"No can do. The only planes in the area are out looking for those kids who were kidnapped."

"You'd better get someone on it right away, Joe. It's going to be a bad one. Over."

There was a brief silence.

"Give me a fix on it. I'll have Cap go over and look at it with the *Island Queen.* He and Carl Orlis are over there in that area, anyway, looking for those kids. I had them on the radio half an hour ago. Over and out."

The forest ranger switched the radio frequency to that of the *Island Queen* and gave her call numbers.

* * *

The boys had been standing near the fire for about half an hour when they heard the sound of a motor in the distance.

"What's that?" Doug asked. "A plane?"

"Could be!"

Phil started to run. "Come on! We've got to get down to the beach so we can signal them when they fly over us!"

The sound of the engine continued to build as they plunged headlong through the brush. It was so close that they thought it must be almost overhead a few seconds before they reached the beach. They stared frantically skyward, waving their arms and shouting to the wind.

"Here we are! Here we are!"

Slowly Doug stopped waving.

"There isn't any plane." His voice was numb. "I don't know how we could be so dumb. That isn't a plane engine!"

"How do you know?" Del asked.

"Just listen to it–It–it's a boat!"

"Bart and his buddies!" Doug murmured.

But the motor wasn't an outboard, they could tell that. Phil's lips parted slightly as he stared through the trees.

"Cap and the *Island Queen!*" he cried.

All three of the boys started waving and yelling at the same time. Uncle Carl and Cap spotted them almost immediately. It was only a moment or two before the boat was close enough so the boys could shout out to her.

"Hi!" The boys grinned.

"Are you all right?" Anxiety still clouded Uncle Carl's voice.

"We are now!" the boys answered.

"Thank God!" Carl said prayerfully.

"We came to investigate that fire," Cap said. "Did you boys start it?"

"Yeah," Doug answered. "We thought that would be the only way anybody would ever find us."

"That was a good idea," Cap said. "Now, put it out, and we'll get on our way."

After trampling the fire out, the boys waded out and clambered aboard the *Island Queen.*

As Cap put the boat into reverse and backed out to deep water, the boys plied him and Uncle Carl with questions. They wanted to know how the two men happened to find out so soon they had been kidnapped and how they happened to be near the island where they had been held captive.

"With all of the islands in the Lake of the Woods I figured we'd be out here a month or two before you or anyone else found us." Phil said.

Cap laughed. "I suppose I ought to keep it a secret; it makes a better story that way. Actually, we just had to do a little minor detective work after Mrs. Braisted saw someone take you boys away in one of the boats."

"You see," Carl broke in, "we figured that you'd caught someone stealing a boat and that your kidnappers must be the bank robbers who were going into Canada. We took a chart and found the closest way to Canada without going through the customs, and that took us this way."

"But," Cap added, "if you guys hadn't started that fire so that Joe saw it at the fire tower, we'd have gone right by that island."

Phil pulled himself up as he remembered the men who had held them captive.

"Hey! What about those guys who stuck up the

bank? We aren't going to let 'em get away with it, are we?"

Doug stared at him. "You aren't thinking we ought to grab them ourselves, are you?"

"Somebody's got to do it before they get that gas line fixed and get away."

Doug shuddered. "Are you out of your mind? They've got guns. Remember?"

The boys looked at Uncle Carl and Cap.

"I'm with Doug this time," Uncle Carl said. "Get on the radio, Cap, and call the RCMP. They'll be able to take care of those guys a lot easier than we can."

Cap switched on the radio and gave the call letters, a note of triumph and relief mingling in his voice.

Phil squinted narrowly at Carl and the captain of the *Island Queen*. The color had left his young face, and nervous sweat moistened his forehead. It scarcely seemed possible that they were free and off the island where the bank robbers had left them.

He looked around. At the moment, the *Island Queen* was as inviting as the luxury liners his dad always kidded about going around the world on.

Doug could scarcely wait until Cap quit talking on the radio. He had pressed so close that the older man jabbed him with his elbow each time he moved. But the boy didn't even notice.

"How long do you suppose it'll take the RCMP to get over here and arrest those guys?" he asked when Cap had completed his message.

Carl noted the time. "I suppose they'll have a little delay before they get the airplane refueled and in the air again. After that it shouldn't be more than a few minutes."

Concern dulled the lights in Phil's black eyes.

"Don't you think *we* ought to go over and–and at least watch to see where those guys go, Uncle Carl? It'd be terrible if they got away."

The older man shook his head. "I don't believe the police need our help at this point. Actually, I believe we would just be in the way. The RCMP will take care of them."

Del broke in quickly. "I really wasn't able to do too much to that motor of theirs to knock it out of commission. All they'll have to do is to cut a short piece out of the rubber gas line and they'll be in business again. They'll be able to hide from the plane like they did before."

But Carl was not to be swayed by their reasoning.

"I still say that it's a job for the police. Especially since those characters happen to have guns." He glanced in Cap's direction. "You agree with me, don't you?"

"It's the only thing to do," Cap said. "We might blunder in and foul things up so the men would get away for sure."

Phil sighed his defeat. "Well, if that's the way it's got to be, I guess there's nothing we can do about it."

The waiting of the next half hour was as long as

any waiting the boys had ever done. Every moment or two one or another looked at his watch or asked what time it was. At last, they heard the whine of an airplane in the distance. Phil leaped to his feet.

"Here they come!"

Doug gasped aloud. "I just thought of something. The men in that plane know the general area to look in, but we know almost exactly where Bart and his pals are. Maybe we ought to head in that direction and, if we spot them, we can radio to the plane to come in and pick them up."

The skipper's mouth tightened.

"I think you've got a point – a very good point!"

He started the engine of the *Island Queen* once more and opened the throttle. The packet boat plowed a widening furrow in the placid water. They went around the island, skirting the reef off the point as closely as they dared, and headed north along the other side. The boys were standing in the bow, peering intently across the lake. Del was the first to spot Uncle Carl's stolen boat.

"There they are!" His excited voice sounded above the throbbing engine.

Bart and his companions had heard the RCMP plane and were paddling toward shore as rapidly as they could. The instant they saw the *Queen* they stopped.

The heavy fishing boat came to a halt seventy-five

to one hundred yards from the island. Del turned to Carl.

"What're they doing now?" he asked.

Carl chuckled to himself. "I think they've finally realized that they're licked. They know they don't have a chance of getting away from the RCMP anymore."

Although the little packet boat made no attempt to move closer, it was apparent that the bank robbers knew they were going to be captured. They made no attempt to get away, even when the Canadian Mounties circled and landed beside them.

* * *

The sun was setting when the *Island Queen* finally pulled in to the Orlis dock. Carl had radioed the news home that he and Cap had found the boys and that the RCMP had arrested the bank robbers. Everybody was down on the dock when the *Island Queen* came in. For a few minutes the scene was the same as it had been when they first arrived three weeks before. Everyone was laughing and talking at once.

Marie threw her arms around her brother, Phil, and hugged him impulsively.

"Hey!" he cried. "What's the big idea?"

He tried to pull away. He was glad to see her, that was true – as glad as she was to see him. But there were all those people around and–and after all, she was just his *sister!* Still, when he saw that there were tears furrowing her cheeks, he put his arms around her clumsily and tried to comfort her. "Don't get so upset, Marie," he said. "I'm home now, and I'm all right. Don't cry so hard."

Mary Orlis was the one who remembered that the boys probably hadn't had much to eat all day. And when she learned that it was true, she herded them in the direction of the house.

"We'll have to go in and find something to eat," she said. "I'm sure you must be starved."

Del answered for all of them. "I'm starved now, but to tell you the truth, I've been too scared all day to think about eating."

"Well, you're not scared now. Come on in the house, and we'll fix you something to eat."

"One minute, please," Edith Braisted broke in crisply.

Startled, the boys stopped. A split heartbeat later, a flash went off a few feet in front of them.

"What was that?" Doug demanded. "What was that?"

The woman laughed musically.

"I was taking your picture for our article."

The boys eyed her curiously. She saw the questions and made explanation as they went into the house.

"I just confessed to Mrs. Orlis and Kay and the girls," she said. "I'd just as well tell the rest of you too."

"Tell us what?" Phil asked.

She waited until they were once more inside the house before continuing.

"First of all, my name isn't Edith Braisted. It's Edith Wilson, and Charlie's my husband."

The boys gasped.

"We're sorry we had to deceive you, but we're a husband-and-wife writing team. I handle the photography and Charlie does the writing. Our editor wanted an article about the Angle, but he insisted that we come up here without letting anyone know who we were or what we were doing. He wanted us to get a completely unbiased picture of the place and the people."

There was a brief silence.

"And to think that I got so annoyed about your 'ball games' so early in the morning that I was about to leave without finishing the assignment."

"And then you found out it wasn't us at all," Doug told her. "It was that crow of Del's."

His brother's cheeks flushed crimson. "That stupid Blackie. I get so mad at him sometimes."

Mrs. Wilson retorted quickly. "I don't think you've got any reason to be mad at him. I find him delightful."

Del's eyes rounded. "You–you do?"

"In fact, I plan to do a feature story of him when we finish the other assignment. I think our readers would be charmed by a picture story of a talking crow."

Del's grin broadened. "Old Blackie is all right at that, but he sure gets me into a jam once in a while."

"But who's Ralph White?" Phil asked. "And why were he and your husband so anxious to stay out of sight when the *Island Queen* came in?"

Mrs. Wilson laughed.

"Ralph is our editor and he and my husband have gone up to Oak Island on the *Island Queen* a number of times. They were afraid they would be recognized by Cap or Kenny Stearns and blow the whole deal."

"I suppose there's a simple explanation for Marcel, too. He was afraid of being seen," Doug put in.

The woman's smile faded.

"Ralph White made friends with Marcel on one of his earlier trips and let Marcel talk him into including him in the trip up here. Marcel didn't want to be seen because he had left home without telling his parents where he was going. When the men found out, they took him back. That's why they left the night before you were captured by those bank robbers. They took Marcel back to Warroad." She paused. "Any other questions?"

"I have one," Mary Orlis put in. "You're actually such an agreeable person, I'm surprised that you were so upset when the RCMP stayed for dinner."

"You may not believe this, but I wanted to see if you're for real."

"What do you mean?"

"You're so sweet and kindly that I had the

impression you were putting on a front for your guests. I wanted to see how you would act if someone was rude and ill-mannered."

"Is that the reason you acted so mad when Blackie woke you up in the morning?" Del asked.

A strange look crossed Mrs. Wilson's face and her cheeks colored.

"I'm afraid I really was rude and ill-mannered on those occasions. Will you forgive me?"

"I can't say that I blame you. That stupid Blackie was enough to irritate anybody."

It was far later than usual when they went to bed that night. But, in spite of the lateness of the hour, Marie was in no hurry to turn out the light.

"Aren't you glad the boys got home safely, DeeDee?" she asked.

DeeDee's pretty, young face grew tender.

"I don't think I ever prayed so hard for anyone since–since." She stopped. She was about to say that she hadn't prayed so hard for anyone since her mom and dad were missing, but she couldn't bring herself to say that, even to Marie. Somehow, thoughts of her parents were almost sacred. She thought about them a lot, but she didn't mention them to anyone except maybe Kay or Danny once in a while.

Marie flashed out of bed and came over to her.

"I've always felt sort of funny about praying for things," she said, "or hearing people pray – until today. But I don't know how I could have stood it if it hadn't been for you and Aunt Mary and Kay asking God to take care of Phil and keep him from harm."

DeeDee nodded. If she were as honest as Marie at that moment, she would have had to admit that praying hadn't meant as much to her the last few weeks as it should have meant. And once in a while she, too, had been embarrassed at hearing someone pray earnestly for something – the sort of prayer that came from the heart. She hadn't felt that way when she had been alone or with other Christians, so much. It was only when Sandy was around, like during evening devotions at home. It made her ashamed of herself.

She looked at her watch. It was almost midnight. She was about to remind Marie of that fact when her cousin scooted closer to her on the side of the bed. It was obvious that she wanted to talk about something but was uncertain how to go about it. At last, she cleared her throat.

"What would have happened to the boys if–if something had happened to them today so they–they didn't get back?"

DeeDee's gaze met hers. "They'd have gone to heaven." She spoke simply, but with authority. This was one thing she had convictions about.

Marie nodded, her face growing even more serious.

"What would happen to us if–if we went to sleep tonight and–and didn't wake up?"

DeeDee thought for a moment. She wasn't entirely

sure just what Marie was thinking about, but she had to answer her honestly.

"I would go to heaven."

That news didn't seem to startle her cousin, but her concern deepened.

"Do you mean that I wouldn't go to heaven?" she asked. "Is that what you're trying to tell me?"

DeeDee searched for words. "Danny says that there is only one way we can know if we're going to heaven or not."

Marie licked her lips with the tip of her tongue.

"He says that Jesus Christ made a claim on the life of each of us when He died on the cross to save us. He wants us to become Christians and–and to be with Him in heaven." She paused significantly. "But we have to meet the conditions. The Bible says that we are all sinners and need saving."

"I–I haven't been so bad."

"The Bible says that 'all have sinned, and come short of the glory of God.' And in another place it says, 'the wages of sin is death.' So we're all sinners and deserve to die."

"Even if we've never done anything real bad?"

DeeDee was silent for a moment or two. "We may not have robbed a bank," she continued, "or stolen anything or gotten drunk or used drugs, but we've envied what other people have, we have told things that weren't true, and we haven't loved the Lord our God with all our strength and with all our mind.

So there are three of the ten commandments we've all broken. And we haven't loved our neighbors as ourselves or honored our parents the way we really should. Have we?"

Marie flushed. "When you put it that way, I guess I have done a lot of things I shouldn't. I guess I am a sinner."

"But the Bible says we don't have to pay the penalty for our sin. Jesus already has done that – He died on the cross for us. So, all we have to do is to tell God that we are sinners and that we want Jesus to save us and help us to live our lives the way Christians should."

"And–and He'll do it?" Marie asked incredulously.

"He'll do it. All you have to do is to ask Him to."

As DeeDee and Marie knelt, a strange exultation swept over DeeDee. She had never before known the joy of pointing a soul to Christ – and especially someone she loved as much as she loved her cousin Marie.

THE
DANNY ORLIS
SERIES

The Danny Orlis series, by Bernard Palmer, delivers a blend of adventure, mystery, and suspense through various settings—from the Canadian wilderness to Guatemalan jungles. Danny Orlis, an adept outdoorsman, skilled athlete, and committed Christian, employs his quick thinking, calm bravery, and biblical solutions to confront everyday problems and hair-raising dangers. Early stories focus on Danny navigating school life, sports, and outdoor challenges, while in later books, Danny and his wife Kay provide wisdom and guidance to youngsters facing lifelike situations and challenges. Having sold over two million copies, this series has made Palmer a renowned author in Christian youth literature. Palmer is also the author of the Felicia Cartright series and various other series for Christian youth.

AVAILABLE FROM WWW.ANEKOPRESS.COM

* 9 7 9 8 8 8 9 3 6 0 6 0 5 *